The Shell

G000114734

The Shell

and Other Stories

COLIN BARKER

Copyright © 2016 Colin Barker

The moral right of the author has been asserted.

Apart from any fair dealing for the purposes of research or private study,
or criticism or review, as permitted under the Copyright, Designs and Patents
Act 1988, this publication may only be reproduced, stored or transmitted, in
any form or by any means, with the prior permission in writing of the
publishers, or in the case of reprographic reproduction in accordance with
the terms of licences issued by the Copyright Licensing Agency. Enquiries
concerning reproduction outside those terms should be sent to the publishers.

This is a work of fiction. Names, characters, businesses, places, events
and incidents are either the products of the author's imagination
or used in a fictitious manner. Any resemblance to actual persons,
living or dead, or actual events is purely coincidental.

Matador
9 Priory Business Park,
Wistow Road, Kibworth Beauchamp,
Leicestershire. LE8 0RX
Tel: 0116 279 2299
Email: books@troubador.co.uk
Web: www.troubador.co.uk/matador
Twitter: @matadorbooks

ISBN 978 1785891 816

British Library Cataloguing in Publication Data.
A catalogue record for this book is available from the British Library.

Printed and bound by CPI Group (UK) Ltd, Croydon, CR0 4YY
Typeset in 11pt Aldine401 BT by Troubador Publishing Ltd, Leicester, UK

Matador is an imprint of Troubador Publishing Ltd

To Carel and Lis.

To Sandy,

With all good wishes,

Colm.

MAY 5t 2019.

———

CONTENTS

The Shell 1

Leslie and Grace Take a Ride 7

The Launch 13

Per Ardua Ad Astra 17

The Rendezvous 23

La Dolce Vita 29

One More Chance 37

The Spider 43

The Passenger 47

Getting up, Getting on 53

The Caretaker 59

The Kite and the Clouds 65

One Last Look 75

The Choice 81

Falling in Love 89

Beyond the Field   107

The Ends of the Earth   115

Hawaii   121

The Well   131

Dishonour Amongst Thieves   143

The Flat   155

Beyond the Grave   179

THE SHELL

High on a rocky promontory jutting into the bay south of Colombo sits the Imperial Hotel, in colonial times formal and grand. Now this grandeur has largely disappeared, but somehow the place still holds a lingering appeal for well-off Sri Lankans with traditional tastes, who hold their family weddings there, rather than use the cosmopolitan hotels in the capital.

There's a large private beach for the use of guests, but it's not one where soft waves lap warm sand whilst a gentle breeze cools the skin. In the nerve-fraying humidity and harsh tropical light, the wind constantly sandblasts the scorching beach, whipping coarse particles into a gritty frenzy. From late morning the sand is too hot to walk in bare feet, and the white breakers, pounding the shore, have a vicious undertow making swimming hazardous.

One part of the beach is set back from the shoreline, and here guests can relax in the shade of dull-green succulents and scruffy battered palms. Eager boys race to fetch loungers and, if they're lucky, one in ten of the holidaymakers gives them a tiny coin. But undaunted, and without charge, they keep the fearless house crows away, reflecting the sun into the birds' eyes with pocket mirrors.

Siri has traded on the hotel's beach for thirty-five of his forty years, peddling shells that no one wants, but day after day he still trudges up and down the beach, humping his heavy tray. When people buy his wares it's out of pity, and vacated hotel rooms often contain his cowries and cones, periwinkles and horn shells. These days he's feeling old and tired, and on a sweltering September day, with the monsoon looming, the beach seems unending and the spiteful sand more abrasive than ever. At noon the temperature reaches forty degrees in the shade, and Siri isn't walking in the shade. Nowadays he finds he has to stop more and more often, and there's a pain in his chest that he puts down to age. He doesn't know the truth, and that's a mercy, for he has no money, and the best he can hope for is that the heart attack, when it comes, will be swift and fatal.

But in the meantime he must work to eat, and he's worried to death. Youngsters, selling stolen scarves and cheap necklaces, are taking his living away, and he's no match for them. Like the house crows, they're clever and relentless, bantering with young foreigners in several languages, and weakening the resistance of older guests with their merciless badgering. Siri would never use such means, even if he could, but his shells seem to be getting smaller and more difficult to sell. He gets them from his well-off brother-in-law Nahil, who has a fishing boat, and makes sure his gentle, trusting relative doesn't know that the best go to expensive shops in Colombo.

Siri can remember a time when hotel guests were well-dressed, courteous and formal, but now that's all in the past. He's observed Europeans all his life, without much curiosity, and senses that deep changes have come about in that far-off place. The new guests are scruffy and fat, coarse, noisy and rude, and spend most of their money on alcohol. To make matters worse, as the monsoon nears and temperatures rise, hotels lower their rates and the clientele really hits rock bottom. These guests aren't interested in shells or charity and Siri's feeling the pinch. So is his brother-in-law, and when he has to tighten his belt, others in his power get squeezed, too.

Siri pays rent to live in a small room in Nahil's family house and he wants him out, pretending that his sister needs the room and she's a blood relative, whereas Siri's only connection with

2

the family was through his dead wife. Siri heard the news before he left for the beach, and Nahil took the opportunity to tell him that he'd no longer supply him with shells. That was so cruel and thoughtless.

Siri was shocked by the utter brutality. He'd kept his room clean and tidy, even spending some of his own money on doing it up, and had always been polite to his sister's family. And by going without himself, he'd bought small presents for the children. How hard it had been to keep smiling when he heard them laughing about his cheap gifts behind his back, and commenting on how worn his clothes had become.

The day is scorching and by three in the afternoon the heat and humidity wrap everything in a crushing embrace. Siri, still deep in shock, oblivious to his physical suffering, trails along the beach, past hotel guests lying in the shade on their sunbeds, drinking colourful cocktails, garnished with fruit.

"Wot you got there, mate?" shouts one of the men to him.

Siri walks shyly over to the group. The speaker is a burly, shaven-headed, tattooed man wearing a baseball cap that says 'Guv' above its peak. Siri kneels down in the sand, and the man leans forward from his lounger, and peers unsteadily at his tray.

"That all you got? Pathetic! I could get bigger shells than that myself," he scoffs and, turning away, loses his balance and grabs at Siri's tray to steady him. Shells erupt into the air and cascade onto the beach, and everyone falls about laughing. Siri's shoulders are shaking, too.

Only a plump, blotchy girl, wiping away her tears, suddenly notices that he's crying. "'elp 'im someone," she cries.

"They're 'is shells, he can fuck off," replies Guv, in a quiet voice. The others sense the menace in his tone, the mirth fades away and, in the sudden silence, only the distant drumming of the surf can be heard. Siri carefully collects up his shells, and finding one missing, looks up at Guv who's glaring down at him. There's a light touch on his shoulder.

"Sorry, darlin'," says the girl softly. "'e's a bit touchy, best leave it at that," and tucks a fifty-rupee note into his breast pocket.

Guv turns his back, grinning at the others who sink back on their loungers, guffawing. Siri walks on, the pain in his chest so bad that several times he has to stop and rest. He leaves the beach early and, when he reaches home, climbs slowly up the back stairs to his room. Once inside, he sees a large cardboard box on the bed.

He has few possessions, but those he has are priceless. He looks around for the little statue of Buddha, which he always kept on his bedside table, but it's missing and so is his father's watch, his mother's ring, and the faded photo of his wife. The pain in his chest comes back, stronger than ever, and he sits down until it passes. He looks inside the cardboard box and finds that his few clothes have been roughly thrown in, and on top of them are the missing items. Breathing heavily, he takes them out and tenderly handles each one, softly kissing the photo of his wife. Then he replaces the Buddha in its accustomed place, kneels before it and prays quietly for several hours.

When he's finished he picks up his few precious items and puts them in a plastic bag which he secures with a cord. Then he carefully cleans the room, places the rest of his belongings in the cardboard box and carries it outside. He hands it, together with the fifty-rupee note, to the beggar who sits on the street corner, returns to his room, ties the plastic bag to his wrist, and walks back down the stairs. He doesn't look back, and there's nothing of him left in the room he has called home for six years.

Evening falls swiftly in Sri Lanka, and down on the dark beach the dazzling surf is pounding away, hurling bitter salt spray into the hot, humid air. Ragged clouds scud across the face of the moon and red flags, flapping furiously, warn that swimming in the heaving sea is very dangerous.

No one sees Siri cross the beach, nobody notices him kneeling on the beach, searching amidst the churned up sand, and there are no witnesses to report what he finds. He turns to face the sea, walking towards the wild breakers and holding out the plastic bag he's taken from his wrist. The heavy waves crash down and then retreat, and to Siri they seem like old friends, eager to embrace him and wash away all the pain he's suffered on the uncaring land. He opens his palm and looks at the shell to give him the strength and will to go on, and moves forward, holding the few things that mean everything to him. He's suddenly aware that he's now as rich as anyone living or dead, for does anyone have more than this at the end?

The first icy shock of the water sends a jet of fire into his chest, then another and suddenly he's gone, without a word or a cry. The sea, his mother, who has received from him what he's offered, spreads herself around her child, a moving shroud in the welcoming darkness.

High above the beach the lights of the hotel gleam brightly, and the after-dinner quiet descends, as it had done countless times before. While below, the sea has returned Siri's body to the land, where it lies on the sand, a shell clasped firmly in the right hand. Those who found him were puzzled: they thought it must have been important to him in some way, but as it seemed so small and ordinary it was hard to see why.

Leslie And Grace Take a Ride

"I wish you'd never seen the car in the first place." Grace, perched in the passenger seat, wrung her hands and bit her lip. "Whatever made you get it, Leslie?"

"Don't worry, love," replied her husband. "It's a Fiesta, and that means it's reliable, easy to drive and cheap to run. And it keeps its value, too." He changed gear with a dull clunk, accelerated with a jerk, and, half turning towards Grace with a smile of reassurance, brushed lightly past a woman with a pram halfway across a pedestrian crossing.

"Oh, be careful, Leslie!" Grace eyes were wide open with alarm. "You can't even drive it properly!"

"I've been driving for over half a century, old girl," said Leslie, cheerfully.

They were coming to a busy roundabout with fast-moving traffic feeding in from their right, and Leslie, sitting bolt upright and peering intently ahead, changed down into the wrong gear. The engine revved loudly, the bodywork shook like a wet dog, and they lurched into the inner lane and then back into the outer, just as a large red car approached the roundabout at speed.

The car was a Mercedes Benz S 63 AMG, with a mighty

V8 engine with all the trimmings. From its steel-sprung struts to its feather-light air suspension, it was a special car for a special person. And its owner, Hugo Jaeger, was just such a one: a millionaire property developer in a chalk-striped suit from Savile Row, a customised shirt from Chris Smith and black Lobb loafers. A young man on the move and one in a hurry, or had been. He'd just heard from his secretary on his hands-free phone that the client he was due to lunch with in the City had cancelled the meeting. Swearing and banging a clenched fist on the steering wheel, he surged towards the roundabout. Suddenly, in front of him, appeared a small blue car, driven by some old fool wearing a Robin Hood hat, sitting upright, staring straight ahead, and chatting to his passenger.

With a roar of rage, Hugo jammed on the ventilated disc brakes with their six piston calipers on the front wheels and rammed his hand on the horn. This caused the other driver to start violently and veer back to the original lane on his right, forcing a motorcyclist to swerve and crash into the prickly shrubs planted in the central island. The small car then crossed back to the outside lane, and shot off at the next exit, before weaving its way along a suburban road. Boiling with rage, Hugo swung the great Mercedes round and set off in pursuit.

After five minutes, Grace looked out of her rear-view mirror. "I think there's a big red car following us," she said.

"Don't be silly, dear. Why would he do that?" said Leslie, wondering why the road he'd turned into, although entirely typical of any in a London suburb, also managed to be utterly unfamiliar. Glancing in his mirror for some clue to their location, he saw that a big red car did indeed seem to be close behind. After another half a mile it was still there, and he began to feel anxious. Grace seemed quiet and looking across at her he saw her hands were clenched, and her eyes were tightly closed. He felt puzzled, but protective.

"Don't worry, dear," he said. "I'll shake him off," and

suddenly turned off to the right, causing a postman to leap for the pavement, scattering his bundle of letters and packages. Meanwhile Hugo, now beginning to enjoy himself, tore down a tree-lined avenue behind the Fiesta and into a cul-de-sac, where he swung the great Mercedes sideways and blocked the little blue car.

Leslie turned off the engine, and in the sudden quiet looked fixedly ahead, his face pale. Grace sobbed into a small handkerchief, and began trembling, and he put a reassuring hand on her arm. "Don't worry, dear, it'll be all right," he said, winding down his window.

Hugo slammed the door of his car and strode towards them. When he reached their car he leaned on the roof and glowered down at Leslie. "I hope you've learned your lesson, you old fool," he said. "If you can't drive any better than that, keep off the bloody road, and stay off it. Just be thankful you cut-up someone reasonable like me, and not some thug who'd have beaten your brains out. Not that I would have blamed him."

Leslie looked up, his eyes wide and frightened. "I'm sorry for what happened, sir," he said, in a small voice, "and now we're in a bit of bother."

"Bother? What sort of bother?"

"Truth to tell, sir, what with you following us and taking on so, I don't feel I can go on driving at the moment. Not with my heart condition. And you've really upset Gracie."

"So get a cab."

"I've no money for taxis, sir, and my wife's sister's very poorly, and she's in hospital. We've got to see her, as soon as possible, sir. Won't you please drop us off at a bus-stop? Any one on the main road will do. It won't take you out of your way. We'd appreciate it so much, and my boy can pick up the car, later."

"Oh, very well," snarled Hugo, looking at his gold Rolex watch. "Get into the back, the pair of you, and at the nearest bus-stop out you go. Understand? I'm not a bloody taxi service."

"Thank you so much, sir," said Leslie, helping the weeping Grace out of the Fiesta and into the Mercedes.

"And keep your hands off the upholstery," said Hugo, over his shoulder, as they moved smoothly away. The big car purred quietly along, but as they drove along the main road a pinging noise started coming from the dashboard.

"God dammit!" shouted Hugo, banging the steering wheel. "I forgot about the damned petrol, you'll just have to wait while I get some fuel."

There was a filling station on the opposite side of the road and they pulled across and drew up on the forecourt. Hugo filled up the car, and went to the pay desk, leaving Leslie and Grace in the back. There was a short queue, which irritated him, but soon he was paying for the petrol with his credit card.

"Nice car that," said the friendly Indian cashier. "Costs a bit to run, though, I'll bet."

Hugo nodded and gestured impatiently for his card.

"Bit old for a chauffeur isn't he, guv?" said the attendant, cheerfully. "Still, suppose he knows what he's doing. Whoops... nearly had those dustbins over... and just missed that lorry, crossing the road."

Hugo whirled round and, seeing the forecourt empty ran out of the shop, catching a glimpse of the Mercedes as it disappeared down the road. "Fucking hell!" he screamed, snatching for his mobile, before he realised he'd left it in the car.

"Soon get the hang of this," said Leslie, staring in wonder at the vast array of dashboard lights, winking and glowing before him.

"I don't believe you've done this," said Grace, who'd dried her tears. "Just what do you suppose Derek will say when we turn up with this? Where's he going to put it? The one you got yesterday is still in the big garage, being repainted, and he's run out of number plates, too."

"He'll be pleased," said Leslie. "He's a good son. Now listen, Gracie, this is important. Where did we leave the Fiesta? If we can't find it we're in big trouble – our fingerprints are all over it. You can drive it to Derek's when we find it, and I'll follow in this. But we've got to get a move on, or it'll be gone! What a world we live in! You just can't trust anyone these days!"

THE LAUNCH

"Can't we launch her soon, Trevor?" Cynthia asked, glancing at the boat on the hard standing, resting on its wooden trestles and shrouded beneath a heavy tarpaulin. There was a chilly breeze coming off the river that May morning, and she was missing the glass of sherry and dry biscuit she took mid-morning in order to maintain her blood sugar level. She tapped her foot impatiently and winced, for Trevor her husband, had bought her shoes on eBay to celebrate the occasion, and they were as ill-fitting as they were unfashionable.

"Nearly there, dear." Trevor smiled, sweeping back the covering on the boat. " We'll drink a toast to her now, but let's be quick – I didn't get enough bubbly for three." From a scuffed tartan duffle bag he produced a half-bottle of Cava, and two long-stem glasses with the filling station price-tags still attached. Handing a glass to her, he attacked the cork using his Swiss Army knife, and the sparkling, shaken wine exploded over Cynthia's designer jeans. She screamed, stepped back and dropped her Louis Vuitton bag onto the hard concrete, their best cut-glass champagne flutes tinkling sharply as they broke against the bottle of vintage champagne she'd brought as a surprise.

"Steady on, old girl," her husband laughed, holding out a steadying hand, which Cynthia snatched away. She began dabbing furiously at her drenched jeans, while Trevor made to speak, but then relapsed into a thoughtful silence. After a while he said, "I wonder what's holding Errol up?"

Before his wife could reply, Pommard, her miniature poodle, an anxious creature, began relieving himself on Trevor's highly polished brogues. He steered it away with a friendly but clumsy foot, and the tiny animal began trembling violently, uttering a litany of well-honed howls. Cynthia snatched up the pulsating bundle, showering kisses on its curly head, and began gathering her things together.

"Hallo, Cynthia! Morning skipper!" boomed a cheerful voice. "Sun below the yardarm already, I see. A bit early, but I'll not say nay."

"Accident with the bubbles, Errol, old man," said Trevor, hurriedly stuffing the bottle of Cava into the duffle-bag, "I wouldn't lean on that thwart, brother mine, you don't know where it's been! But I do. Don't worry a touch of turps'll soon get rid of that nasty mark."

"I wore this specially for today," said Errol, in an injured tone scrubbing at the oil stain on his jacket, and redistributing it generously over his person.

"Sorry, sorry, sorry," Trevor muttered, moving on. "Let's proceed to the launch. Errol, you haul the bows and I'll push from the stern. We'll *poise* it by the water and then, one good heave and we'll be afloat!"

His brother bent to the task, but in spite of his warning shouts, found himself precipitated into the water by the potency of Trevor's thrust. When he regained dry land, his desert boots were shedding squeaky water and his cavalry twill trousers were clinging around his calves with a vice-like grip.

Cynthia wondered how long all this was going to take. She'd unwisely agreed to meet Sharon Hogg, her beauty consultant that morning, and suspected that she'd be already tackling her first glass of chilled chardonnay in Fergal O'Brien's Ceilidh Carvery. It was unlike anywhere else Cynthia ever visited and she only went at Sharon's insistence. But how she relished the response she received from the heavy-booted, sweat-stained clientele. 'Feral beasts,' she'd murmur to herself, biting her lip, her pulses racing, lapping up the lascivious glances of the rough building trade. Sitting there, high on a bar-stool and showing her slim legs to advantage, she felt like a princess amongst frogs, secretly assigning Sharon a place in the same amphibian family.

Trevor's blood pressure was also rising elsewhere, as he sought to divert Errol's attention to the launch, rather than simply cursing whilst shaking his leg to loosen the damp embrace of his trousers.

"One more effort and she'll be away!" he shouted. "Now, both together!"

But Errol's good humour was soon to be sorely tried, yet again. Having moved amidships to promote the final lunge he slipped and fell heavily. One of his jacket pockets caught in the boat's starboard rowlock, and was ripped to shreds.

"Bugger, *bugger!*" he shouted, losing his grip and grabbing at the amputated flap, while all his small change and other precious objects poured down onto the concrete.

"Steady on, Errol," said Trevor sternly, "ladies present."

"Not for much longer," said Cynthia, tossing her head, and unwittingly throwing the glowing half of her daily-allowed cigarette onto a pile of oily rags beneath the boat. "I'm not staying here to hear language like that!" She steamed off at full speed, thereby missing the drama unfolding in her wake.

When the firemen had extinguished the flames, Trevor looked sadly at the charred remains of their boat. The gently smoking ribs, blackened and bare, resembled a rack of lamb he'd once sent back several times in a restaurant, before his premature eviction from the premises. Errol, who'd used his jacket to help beat out the flames, stood in silent empathy with his brother, the scorched remnant dangling from his heedless hand.

"We never even got it into the water," Trevor sighed.

"Meant to be," Errol replied, "meant to be."

"What a blaze, though," said Trevor. "You don't get heat like that from a badly built boat."

Errol smiled, relishing the comfort of his stiff, fire-dried trousers. "I call that a proper Viking funeral," he said, "a fitting end for a well-found vessel!"

Meanwhile Cynthia, perched on her bar-stool, a little guilty now at abandoning the launch, and unaware of her part in the boat's incineration, was thinking about cruising down the river, trailing her hand in the water and sipping champagne. But what to wear? Thoughtfully, she sipped a little more wine.

Elsewhere, in the 'Lamb and Limpet,' the brothers, their spirits bolstered by several pints of Wreakers' Ruin, were looking to the future.

"Water's finished, in my book," said Trevor.

"Nasty, over-rated stuff," Errol replied.

"The open sky!" Trevor's voice had taken on the evangelical note that thrilled Errol. "Where a man's dreams can take off, and have some room to grow."

"Some *space*," said Errol.

Trevor glanced at his empty beer mug. "Looking into the flames this morning, I saw it all, as plain as day. Rockets! Your round, I believe, Errol."

His brother sought the bar, brow furrowed and mind full of empty space. And by the time he had returned, Trevor had not only sketched out the body of a prototype rocket on a coaster, but christened its launching pad as well. 'Cape Cynthia,' was born that day, and toasted in nut-brown ale. But how the source and inspiration of the name reacted to the heart-felt honour remains a closely guarded secret to this very day.

PER ARDUA AD ASTRA

C ynthia inspected her slim, tanned legs with composure and her shoes with affectionate irritation. The little felt caps on their tiny heels, designed by her husband, might protect the exposed floorboards in their sitting room but were hardly fashionable in the footwear department. What could she say? Tender thought had gone into their conception, and care and ingenuity in their construction and fitting.

"There's a lot to be said for practical husbands," she said, turning to Sharon, her beauty consultant, lounging on a bar seat in her kitchen. "Trevor's good like that, but not what you'd call *romantic*. Clever and thoughtful, though... for a man, that is."

Sharon, who was studying the *OK! Magazine* she always carried around with her, took another swig of Campari and soda, and muttered something unintelligible. The way she'd turn up unannounced, always expecting a drink, really annoyed Cynthia.

"Now he's building a rocket in the garden shed, and his brother Errol's there to help him," Cynthia continued. "That's his old motorbike propped up by the shed, not exactly decorative, is it?"

Sharon, bored with reading about celebrities, squinted out of the window. "What's that sign on the shed door say, Cynth?" she asked.

"*Per Ardua ad Astra.*"

"Through struggle to the stars. How quaint," said Sharon.

Cynthia gave her a quick look, but Sharon didn't react, and went on examining her nails. Happy with what she saw, she glanced again at the garden. "Just look at that!" she said.

What had caught her eye was a twisting plume of orange smoke gushing from the stack-pipe on the shed's roof, which thickened and grew black and oily as they watched in amazement. From inside the shed they then heard a muffled crash, some loud shouts and what sounded like swearing. Next minute Trevor and Errol stumbled out of the shed and hurled themselves towards the house. They were big men, and there was a slight hiatus as they passed abreast through a delicate pergola, before leaping over the garden pond and crashing down behind a statue of Patience.

The ample proportions of the stone figure shielded them from the explosion that shattered the shed's roof, hurling heavy timbers like matchsticks high into the air. From the depths of the ensuing fireball, squadrons of garden gnomes, released from their muster on the shelves where they awaited their annual cleaning, took off like ballistic missiles. As they rose into the sky, they fragmented, plummeting into next door's garden like a heavy hailstorm.

Their arrival into Roland Chivers' cucumber frame was accompanied by a shockwave from another explosion that shattered every one of his newly installed, double-glazed bedroom windows. An immense cloud of pungent smoke then surged into the air, with Errol's motorcycle ascending amongst its writhing billows. Roland, blown over by the blast, which whisked away his hairpiece, ended up on his back, covered in the shredded remains of a duvet cover from his wife's washing line. In the lull that followed, a gentle rain of smouldering cinders floated down upon his well-groomed garden, coming to rest amongst the remnants of his wife's spotless laundry hanging out to dry.

Meanwhile, Errol's motorcycle continued upwards on its erratic path, revolving like a giant Catherine wheel and dismembered by periodic explosions. Roland, clutching his naked head and limp with shock, watched the flight-path of the scrap-iron comet with an interest becoming intense, as it began descending towards his driveway and his precious mobile home.

This vehicle, parked behind his garage, combining unmatched utility with an impeccable pedigree, was a priceless 1953 Cherokee de Luxe, outright winner of the *Concours d'Elegance* for six years running at the national convention of 'We Speedy Wayfarers' held at Camber Sands. And this year Roland and Doris Chivers had worked as never before to prepare their champion for the battle of a lifetime. For recently there was a rumour that perennial runner-up, Dudley Brimton, from Tamworth, had uncovered an original Comanche Excelsior, and restored it to perfect condition.

As Errol's incandescent motorcycle crashed to earth, it landed plumb on the roof of the Cherokee and although it immediately slid off, the effect was cataclysmic. There was a flash of eye-searing brilliance and a 'whoomph' as flames engulfed the most celebrated 'home-on-wheels' of its generation, spreading smoking rubber, charred wood and molten plastic over a wide area.

When everything combustible had been consumed in the flames, Trevor and Errol climbed over the remains of the fence, past the smashed cucumber frame and joined Roland, who was standing beside the smouldering pyre in his tattered toga. They stood for a while in silence, and then solemnly shook his hand and returned home, Errol wheeling his blackened vehicle, its single wheel squeaking, whilst their feet grated on ground-up garden gnome and fragments of burnt bakelite.

Some time later, to celebrate the final settlement of the insurance claim, Roland and Doris joined the brothers and Cynthia in the saloon bar of the 'Lamb and Limpet.' "It's no joke, seeing your dreams going up in smoke," said Trevor, taking a pull at his pint of Wreakers' Ruin.

"An ill wind, though," said Roland, wondering why the beer he was drinking, as brown and thick as gravy, tasted like it, too.

"Insurance paying up, you mean?" said Trevor.

"Well that, of course, but really I meant the dear old Cherokee retiring as Champion Motorhome. Unbeaten for six years running. No one can ever take that away from us."

"A blessing in disguise," said Errol, draining his pint.

"'Fiery Fate of a Living Legend'. That's what they said on the front page of the club magazine," Roland said, proudly. "I'm senior vice-president now, a great honour."

"What puzzled us most about the whole thing," mused Trevor, leaning back in his chair and studying the ceiling intently, "was that Errol's bike landed on the Cherokee's roof and bounced off, but the whole thing went up like a blessed napalm bomb."

"As if some *unseen* hand was at work," said Errol, running a moistened finger, around the rim of his empty mug. "And there was that smell of petrol around the place, that very morning."

Trevor nodded, "Petrol smells don't always mean deliberate spills, but you try telling that to an insurance company. That's what we said."

"Same all round?" said Roland, gathering up the empty glasses. "By the way, Errol, if you haven't done anything about it yet, I can put you in the way of a very nice replacement for your motorbike."

"Much obliged, Roland."

"And Cynthia, I'm sure you'd enjoy some of the events 'We Speedy Wayfarers' are planning this year. As senior vice-president's guest, naturally."

"How nice," said Cynthia. "Drop more rum in the Pina Colada next time, please, Roland."

"And don't go buying cucumbers, Trevor. You only have to ask."

"Very generous. Hope the glass we put in your frame is doing the job."

"Yes, most grateful, lads," said Roland. "Must settle up with you, for that, some time. We've got to help each other out in this life, haven't we? Where would we be, if we didn't?"

"Where, indeed," said Trevor, pushing his empty pint pot across the table.

"Any danger of some crisps?" said Errol. "No rush – it's not as if we've got another fire on our hands, is it? Well, not until later, anyway!"

"Don't look so stricken, Roland," Trevor laughed. "It's his idea of a joke, just a little joke! Anyway it's tomorrow he's thinking of, not now!"

THE RENDEZVOUS

Alex fought down the sudden wave of sheer panic but the effort left him feeling faint and horribly sick. The intense feeling passed, but the hand that wiped his sweating forehead was shaking violently. Escape and freedom were getting nearer, but every step was a burden he longed to lay down. But go on he must, for the minutes to the planned rendezvous were ticking away. He didn't like to think about what lay ahead if he missed the deadline, but he knew what it was: capture, torture and death. *You're too old for this*, his aching body cried out, and weakened with constant worry, his mind agreed. But what use was that knowledge to him now? Should he end it? He had the means. But then he thought of his family, and the everlasting hell in store for suicides, and realised that killing himself wasn't an option.

His pursuers, fit and keen, had guns, fierce dogs and the remorseless cruelty of indoctrinated youth. They'd been following him ever since he'd been spotted photographing the airfield. How long ago was that? His tired mind didn't know. He vaguely recalled dumping the car, and then struggling on foot through fens and farmland, and over ditches and dykes. And now he was in this sunken lane, sheltered but not safe. Was there no sanctuary for him anywhere in this damned country?

Peering through a gap in the hedge growing along the top of the earthen bank, he saw a large ploughed field rising towards woodland, the trees outlined against the sky. He hauled himself up from the road, squeezed through the hedge and stood up, breathing hard. There was a rough path running up the side of the field, and he began stumbling along it, only the thought of his capture keeping him moving. After several hundred metres he paused, his heart thumping and his chest heaving. He stared back at the way he'd come and listened, relief flooding over him when he heard nothing. And then his heart dropped, as he realised that silence only meant that the dogs were in the sunken lane, sniffing round to pick up his scent.

After another quarter of a mile of laboured running he'd nearly reached the top of the field, the wood ahead of him and to his right. He noticed there was plenty of undergrowth between the thickly planted trees, which was helpful for hiding, but hard going for a hunted man. He looked around but only saw a long field of stubble, sloping upwards. It would be easier to run here than in the wood, but he'd be much longer in the open. And when they'd spotted him, they'd let loose the dogs to run him down. And then the interrogation would begin, for a spy's confession in this endless cold war was invaluable. He moved towards the wood.

Between the field and the trees was a ditch, and beyond that lay a rusty barbed-wire fence, in places broken and twisted. He scrambled down into the hollow, dived through a gap in the wire, and plunged on through the trees. Glancing over his shoulder as he ran, he saw soldiers climbing up from the sunken lane, their dogs ahead of them. A few hundred metres into the wood and he leant against a tree to get his breath back. The undergrowth was thick here with no paths, and his leather satchel, containing plans and photographs, weighed a ton. Why had he gone back for that unnecessary shot of the airfield? He cursed himself for a fool.

Alex now had thirty minutes to reach the landing strip and board the plane they'd sent to pick him up. He knew it wouldn't wait if he wasn't there, and for some reason his hand went to the pocket where he kept the photo of his family. It was the twins' eighth birthday tomorrow, and he'd promised them he'd share it with them at home. How he longed to see them, and how he loathed this country and everything about it!

He crashed on through the undergrowth and then the trees thinned out and he was in a small clearing. It was late afternoon and the low-slanting sunlight so dazzled him that he blinked and rubbed his eyes. In front of him he saw a stream, swollen by recent rainfall, and a small path leading to a moss-covered, stone footbridge one hundred metres downstream. When he reached it, he stumbled over its loose stones and gained the further bank, running down to the water's edge to judge its depth. He stared for a moment at the stream and its fluid flow, noting there was no noticeable movement in mid-stream where it was deep, but by the margins, twitching sedges betrayed a strong current beneath the calm surface. A little further upstream he saw shallower water running rapidly over a stream-bed of bright pebbles, and then suddenly panicked, feeling exposed now he was no longer shielded by the dark wood.

He hurriedly stepped into the water and waded with the current, planning to push on until he was hidden from the bridge, then leave the stream and follow the fields to the landing site. The sun, red and bloated now, sent shafts of late light through the willow branches by the bank, making moving patterns on the water as he splashed his way against the flow. Beyond the shallows he found the water deepened, a cool breeze skimmed the surface of the stream, and clouds of gnats rose high around him. Another hundred metres on and he heard the dogs barking, and knew he must seek the shelter of the bank. But now the stream had opened out, and its margins had turned into marshland, where cattle came down to drink, and oily water oozed from cloven hoof-prints in the mud.

Alex pushed on, sticking to the firmer, pebble-strewn ground in the middle of the stream-bed, the fresh night air chilling his legs and ankles, and dense swarms of insects swirling round his head. He slapped at them and they jerked away, instantly reforming. Maddened he struck out again, and foolishly lunged after the dancing insects, but they easily eluded him. He reached a spot where a barbed wire fence, stretched across the water, now running rapidly past little white beaches of fine sand. He lowered himself under the wire, soaking his trousers in the water, icy cold, even after a day of sunshine finding the pulse of the current surprisingly strong. The flow tugged urgently at his legs and, looking down he saw a crayfish by his foot, its shape distorted by the water. Instinctively he reared away from the creature, cursing as he fell against the wire and then wrenching his clammy trousers free from the barbs. His legs were badly scratched, and thin skeins of his blood swirled away downstream.

He hauled himself out of the water and onto the overgrown margin of a stubble field of harvested wheat. He stepped forward and something hidden in the grass exploded under his feet causing him to shout aloud in surprise. A partridge whirred away through the dusk, and he gazed in wonder at the crushed grass where the bird had been hiding. Then he heard again the sound of dogs, but coming now from the other side of the stream, their barking fading as they moved away. His heart leapt up for there was just time to get to the landing strip, but he hesitated to run across an open field.

A low ditch ran the length of the field parallel to the stream. Two more fields after this one and he could lie up, and wait for the plane, only breaking cover at the last moment. He jumped down into the ditch and ran swiftly along it, half crouching until he came to a large concrete pipe crossing his path. Dragging himself up the bank, he half fell into the adjacent field, struggled to his feet and disturbed a covey of partridges which surged into the air, with a shocking beating of wings.

As they lifted up, he rose amongst them, almost flying backwards, like an airborne gymnast, his chest and face bloody and lacerated by the point-blank shotgun blast. He fell to earth on his back, his bloodied satchel disgorging its contents high into the air, the photos, papers and maps, flying away towards the stream.

The gunman dropped to his knees with a great cry, and cradling Alex's head in his arms burst into hysterical tears of shock and remorse. He was a local man, going home after a bad day's shooting, petulantly loosing off both barrels at ground-rising birds. Alex lay, feeling strangely peaceful, trying to reach in his pocket for his photographs, but his hands wouldn't work, and he sank back. And as the light dimmed he heard, far-off the sound of a small plane approaching, the pilot cutting back the speed and the noise of its engine as it landed and taxied forward. It paused for a moment before accelerating, taking off and roaring into the distance.

As the noise faded Alex slipped quietly away, and the huntsman, still sobbing and groaning, reached inside his pocket and found the family photo, bloodied and torn. He stared at the words on the back. They said 'Magda, Olga and Ivan, Yalta 1958'. When the soldiers came with their dogs, the man looked up for a moment and then they all gazed down in silence at the broken body on the ground. The darkness crept quietly around them, the field faded from view and the stream flowed gently on.

La Dolce Vita

The sound of bells from the *duomo* wakes Carlo from a deep sleep. He groans and looks around, and as his bleary eyes adjust to the shuttered light he finds he's in an unfamiliar room. He can neither remember getting there last night, nor does he recognise who he's been sleeping with. Terribly hungover, he feels like death, but then jerks wide awake. Bells! Bells mean Sunday, and that means he's late. Panic!

He's pretty sure there'll be no money left after last night. More panic. Sick and dizzy, he retches as he slowly moves his legs out of the bedclothes, careful not to wake the snoring woman. What was her name? Maria? Who knows or cares? He notices how the bright sunlight, streaming through a gap in the shutter, shines on her filthy feet, poking out from the bottom of the shiny nylon sheets, and wrinkles his nose at the smell in the bedroom.

He stumbles around the room, groping for his clothes on the floor in the semi-darkness. It's just as he thought, for when he goes through the pockets of his jeans all he finds is a crumpled empty cigarette packet and a few lire. The woman's clothes strewn across the floor yield nothing, nor is there anything inside her purse on the dressing table. He swears softly to himself and takes a last look around, in the vain hope of seeing something saleable. What a hope!

He opens the door and tiptoes down the steps to the small

piazza below, combing his long, oily hair with a sticky comb as he goes. He kicks the buckled wheel of an ancient moped left leaning against a dusty fig tree, and pushes past a scum-ringed shower tray and some plastic pipes propped against the wall. He's wearing expensive crocodile skin shoes with Cuban heels, and steps gingerly over the stained paving stones, smeared with grease and oil and littered with broken pantiles and empty coke cans. A cat with hungry eyes, dull-furred and dirty, watches him as he walks out onto the Via della Rosa. He picks up a shard of tile to throw at the animal, but can't be bothered, and chucks it away in disgust. He hastens towards the city walls.

These mediaeval brick ramparts form an unbroken loop around the town, but pedestrians may still walk through the narrow, dark tunnels that punctuate the walls at regular intervals. Some have iron portcullises, now rusted and useless, originally designed to keep out intruders, and one such passage leads to the *duomo*, whose towering campanile is easy to spot from the ring-road circling the city. Its entrance is clearly marked and well used by tourists, most of whom are still having breakfast in their hotels as Carlo walks briskly towards it. As he nears the tunnel he hears the noise of running water in the aqueduct parallel to the passageway, flowing swiftly into the darkness, its sound magnified by the confined space through which it runs. And that's precisely why Carlo's here.

The crenellated walls above the tunnel entrance are twenty feet high, and on the path running along the battlements is a large stone figure of a lion. Carlo climbs the steps to the top of the ramparts, and, shielded by the statue, looks over to where a path, running across a wide strip of grass, meets the passage below him. It doesn't take long before he sees her – a lone walker, middle-aged, with shoulder-length grey hair, and a determined pelvic thrust making for the tunnel. American without a doubt, but Carlo's only interest is in the contents of the large handbag slung over her shoulder.

She enters the dim, echoing passage, and Carlo, after glancing around to make sure he's alone, climbs down from the walls, and waits for her in a niche by the mouth of the passageway. There's a slight kink inside before it reaches the open and he knows that she'll be temporarily blinded by the light as she turns the corner. The woman's footsteps coming nearer, sound hard and hollow, but subdued by the noise of the rushing water. When she turns the corner, he pounces on her from the shadows.

He's planned on total surprise, leading to an easy snatch and then swift escape into the maze of streets running off the Corso Garibaldi. But the old cow, spoiling it all, holds on to her bag, shouting, "Help! Let go, you bastard. Help!" So he's no option but to drag her back into the tunnel, still struggling and shouting, where he lunges at her, punching her hard in the face. She gasps with shock, but somehow still manages to keep hold of her bag. Exasperated, he kicks her hard in the stomach, and she crumples up and starts shaking and moaning.

He wrenches the bag from her and rips it open. There's a purse inside with enough lire and dollars for what he needs, and also a syringe. Crafty old bitch, he thinks – and her looking so upright! Some of these foreigners were the pits. He checks her jewellery and finds nothing, except some trashy Indian beads and a metal bracelet round her wrist with writing punched into the surface. Reading isn't his thing but he makes out the words 'epileptic' and 'diabetic,' which don't mean anything to him and the bracelet looks worthless. He wrenches it off her wrist and throws it with her handbag into the fast-flowing water.

The woman is still and quiet now, and he moves her face into the light, to have a better look. Her skin's the colour of putty, and he's relieved for she's no threat to him in this state, and as he'd struck in the dark she couldn't recognise him again. Just to make sure she doesn't cry out too soon he looks around and, finding a dirty plastic bag on the ground, stuffs it into her mouth. After hauling her back into the recess, he props her against the wall, straightens up, brushes down his clothes, and steps out into the Via della Rosa.

He walks in a studied, calm way through the Piazza San Martino and along the Via del Duomo, which leads into the largest square in the old city, the Piazza Napoleone. It's quite empty, and after crossing the square, he breaks into a run, making for the Via Santa Giustina where there's a maze of narrow streets, with steel-shuttered shopfronts. He runs down the street, towards one of these, where the owner, fat, unshaven and wearing a grubby vest, is sitting on a dirty plastic chair, smoking a cigar.

"You little bastard, now what you want?" he says amicably to Carlo, spitting fragments of cigar into the road in front of the young man. "You don't have money, you don't get nothing. You owe for last week."

"I've got money," says Carlo, "for the love of God you got to help me out."

"*Soldi*," says the man, flicking his fingers, and Carlo holds out the lire and dollars.

"All lire next time, or you get fuck all," says the man, taking the money, and getting up with an effort. He unlocks the metal shutter, heaves it up with a clatter, waddles into the lock-up, and comes back with two cardboard boxes. "Now, get the fuck outta here," he says, flopping back onto his chair.

It takes Carlo twenty minutes to reach the flat he shares with his brother, Mario, near the Piazza Santa Maria. He's doing another stretch in a Roman prison, so Carlo's alone. He showers, shaves off three days' growth of beard, and puts on his only clean shirt, the one that his mother gave him for Christmas. He slicks back his thick, black hair, picks up the two parcels and leaves the flat, carefully locking the door.

He has two hours to kill, and makes for his usual bar which has a snooker table upstairs. He'll bum a few cigarettes off someone there, and, if he's lucky, get a mate to buy him a drink. It'll mean doing a job or two in the week for them, but he's thirsty and desperate for a smoke. After two hours he emerges from the smoky snooker parlour, blinking in the strong sunlight, and ten minutes later he's in the Piazza San Agostino, climbing up the steps to his mother's apartment.

There are twenty-two steps and his mother hasn't set foot on one of them for twenty years. Between the first and second floors he meets Gina, his sister, coming down. God, he thinks, she looks like shit – only four years older than him, and she could be his mother. She's a slight, pale woman, with dark-ringed exhausted eyes, short hair and blotchy skin. She stiffens when she sees him. "I've made the lunch," she says, in a tired, angry tone, "it's in the oven. All you have to do is take it out, and serve her. And do you think for once you could do a little washing up? I'll be back later to see if she's all right."

Carlo shrugs; he sees no need to wash up anything. He once tried to imagine what his mates would have said, if they'd burst in on him in a kitchen and found him wearing a pair of yellow rubber gloves. The horror of such a thought has never left him. And to think that he once had the goodness to tell his sister she needed to do something about herself. All she said was how busy she was looking after their mother, her husband, their three kids, and her father-in-law. How can you help people like that? No wonder her old man was out half the night, chasing every bit of skirt he could get his hands on!

He leaves the parcels outside his mother's door and goes inside. It's like walking into an oven, and there's a strong odour of cheap scent, stale cooking, sweat, drains and deep-seated damp. An enormous woman with frizzy, dyed dark hair, her face caked with make-up and her body wrapped in a vast frilly bed-jacket, is propped up in bed in the middle of the living room. On seeing her son, her features break into a radiant smile.

"I'm here to see the sweetest mummy in the world," he cries, advancing towards her with outstretched arms.

"Little Carlo," she screams, holding out her pendulous arms. "Here let me look at you, you lovely boy. No!" she cries in mock seriousness, "not a lovely boy – a great handsome man."

Carlo preens and postures, while she simpers and smirks. "I saw Gina on my way up," he says. "She said that dinner's in the oven. Let me serve you, lovely Mamma."

"You're such a blessing to me," she sighs. "How many sons would help his mother like you do? Left alone to die with hardly a word from that lazy slut, Gina. But has my son nothing for his mother?" Her hard little eyes glitter in their pouches of fat, as she shifts her bulk in the bed, "Or has he forsaken me, too?"

"Is that a knock, I hear?" Carlo cries, crossing to the door. He goes outside and picks up the boxes. "A special delivery," he says, coming back into the room, and pretending to read what's written on the packages. "Addressed to 'The most special person in the world'." And with that he hands her the parcels, which she accepts with delight. It's always the same: a bottle of the best French brandy, and a box of Belgian chocolates. So all's well, and when they've eaten, and he's piled all the greasy plates up in the kitchen for his sister to cope with, he smiles at her.

"And don't think I've forgotten a certain person's birthday," his mother beams at him. "If little Carlo wants to look, he might find something downstairs."

So he rushes down the stairs, opens the door to the lock-up and there, brand new from the factory, is a magnificent racing bicycle, gleaming and sparkling. At last he cries to himself. And then comes a stab of bitter disappointment. It's nearly the best, but not quite the best – and nearly is not nearly good enough. Why couldn't his mother have got it right? He's dropped enough hints to the stupid old cow. But he's playing the long game, and reduces her to floods of hot delighted tears in proclaiming what immeasurable delight the gift has brought him.

Now he can't wait to get into the kit that has come with the bike and take to the road, and his mother, suffused with pleasure, permits an early departure. The bike's a dream, and he rides like a pro. A young, proud, Italian, untroubled and free. There's only him in the whole world, and it was made for him. Life's for the lucky, luck is what you make it, and devil take the hindmost.

He takes the mountain road to Castelnuovo, and pounds on, over the Passo di Radici, high in the Alpi Apuane, flying down the great sweeping downhill run for twenty kilometres towards Lucca. He can't wait to descend to show off the bike, and pedals faster and faster downhill, as if his life depended on it.

But lucky as usual, Carlo doesn't need to wait that long. A split second later, swerving to avoid an oncoming car, he's descending even faster than he dared hope. But this time, and instead of carrying his mother's blessing, he's weighted down with the curse of the family of the dead American woman, and falling straight down to where the granite-hard floor of the river valley waits to welcome him, 200 metres below.

ONE MORE CHANCE

When Luigi and his dad came back from the city that evening, they had the dusty road all to themselves. And as they drove along in silence, with all the country scents seeping in through the open windows of the car, they both felt the strong, unspoken bond between them. They both loved this time of day, and being together always made things extra special.

Luigi was watching a buzzard circling high when his father told him that someone would be in touch with him soon. That was always how things happened: a casual word, hints from an unknown source, rumours turning out to be true, and sometimes certainties never happening. "And if Mr Scaratti, asks you to 'do him a favour'," his father continued, "do *exactly* what he wants. Succeed, and the world's your oyster, but fail and you'll be looking over your shoulder for the rest of your life. And you'll only get one shot at it, don't forget that."

Luigi, who'd just turned seventeen, gulped and nodded. This was real grown-up stuff, and he felt frightened. He desperately needed to confide in Billy, but his big brother wasn't around anymore, and no one would tell him where he was. Was this what it meant to be an adult? He had a terrible feeling that it was. Then he squared up, for this would be his first real job, and he was determined to get it right, for his dad as much as himself.

His father had a good job, and had always been greatly respected and valued by his bosses. But now things didn't seem to be going too well, and at night he heard scraps of conversation between his parents that worried him. "I just can't seem to get it right for them... the court threw out our defence... I think Billy's in trouble... what about you if something happens to me?"

The small town they lived in was near the city where his father worked as an accountant. He was gentle and kind, devoted to his employers, scrupulously thorough in laundering money, and expert at making financial returns appear above board and look legal. He was reticent about his job even to his family, and never ever spoke of it to anyone he didn't know. Luigi didn't want to know, for he'd absorbed the culture in which they lived, where a veneer of respectability was underpinned by bribery, extortion and terror. It was that same culture that paid his dad a handsome salary, met his mother's hospital bills, and would see him through college. Silence sustained the illusion of legitimacy, and helped quieten the conscience of people like his mom and dad.

"When will they ask me?" Luigi was troubled.

"I don't know," said his father, "but they'll ask you as a man, not me as your dad."

"Will I have to *kill* someone," he stammered. "I just *couldn't*."

"Maybe," said his father, surprisingly. "They'll test your loyalty and commitment, and it won't be easy. But don't forget when you pass the test, they'll be totally loyal to you and yours for the rest of your life. Think about that."

"I'll fail, I'll let you down, I'll chicken out!"

"No you won't, and one day soon you'll make me proud to be your father."

Luigi, still at high school, earned money stacking shelves at a local supermarket, and usually finished at seven o'clock. One Saturday, not long after his conversation with his dad, he left by the staff exit as usual and was approached by a boy he didn't know. That was odd, for in his small town most children knew others of the same age, at least by sight, if not by name. The boy was wearing city clothes and a trilby hat, far too big for him.

"You Barrati?" he asked, and Luigi nodded. The boy handed him a piece of paper, tilted his hat and walked away, without a word. The note told him to go the next morning to where a dirt road was crossed by an old railway line. He must be there at 5.00am and alone, and no one must know of the arrangement. He was to bring his mobile phone.

And now here he was. At first he'd felt sick with apprehension, but after smelling the sweet morning air, cool and pleasant under a filmy canopy of dawn clouds, he sensed the stillness, and calmed down. Savouring the relief of just being there after such a sleepless night, he felt ready for anything. Few people other than farmers ever used this road crossing, and, looking around he saw nothing but reddish sand, withered sage bushes, a bone-dry eucalyptus grove and an untidy jumble of sun-bleached rocks. His eye followed the dirt road stretching away beyond the iron track, snaking its way towards low, scrub-green hills, already getting hazy in the distance.

A few minutes later, a large black car drove swiftly up, coming from the road to town, and screeched to a halt in a cloud of dust. The driver switched off the engine, waited until Luigi had walked over to the car, then leant across and released the door catch on the passenger's side. Bending down and peering at the driver, he saw a bulky middle-aged man, already sweating in the rising heat, with a chalk-white, pock-marked face and thick lips, wearing a trilby. The car reeked of stale sweat, and acrid cigar smoke.

"Hiya, kid," the man said. "Get in the passenger seat and I'll show you the controls. Then you can take over." Luigi listened carefully and then walked round the car while the man got out of the driver's seat, and stood waiting for him. Close up, the boy could see the enormous shoulders and large, white hands covered with black hair, the livid scars on his neck and the puckered half-closed eye.

"Ya know the old quarries, over there?" asked the man, pointing along the road. Luigi nodded – the workings, long abandoned, held deep standing water, and he'd spent many hours swimming there with Billy and the bigger boys, when he was younger. "Plastic bag in the trunk, for delivery to the bottom of the lake," said the man. "Heavy. If it moves a bit just get it underwater – that'll soon stop it wriggling!" he laughed. "And no peeking in the bag, strict orders from Mr Scaratti. Also, he said to ring your dad just before you dump the package, something about making him proud. Drive the car back here when you're done."

Luigi climbed into the driver's seat, his heart beating wildly. What a great way to start his first job, and how nice of Mr Scaratti to suggest ringing his father before dumping the black bag. He was suddenly aware of the man looking at him. "You coming too?" he asked.

"Just you, kid," said the man, stepping back, and gestured for him to move on. Luigi adjusted the seat, and started the engine. His first job, and not so hard, after all! He drove away glancing in the rear-view mirror, and saw the man standing in the bright morning sunlight watching him go, impassive and incongruous in his city suit.

Luigi drove carefully along the dirt road leading to the sun-baked foothills, and as the road climbed, the vegetation gave way to cactus and scrub. After a while the way narrowed and split, and taking the smaller track he climbed higher still, now between large, lichen-flecked boulders. After a sharp left-hand bend the road descended steeply, following the tracks of lorries which had once transported thousands of tons of stone from the quarries. Away to his left was a gleam in the bottom of the workings, and a final, steep descent, and the road brought him level with the lake and the glittering water.

He drove the car onto a rocky bank by the water's edge, and turned off the engine. Then, with trembling hands he dialled his father's mobile number, and waited impatiently, his heart beating quickly, eager to tell him what had happened. The phone connected and began ringing, but he sensed at once that something was wrong, for the tone seemed muffled and strangely near. Then he realised that the sound was coming from the trunk of the car, and his heart missed a beat, for his father never went out without his mobile, and it never left him.

Luigi gave a cry and, fumbling with panic, jerked the key out of the ignition, and ran to the back of the car. With shaking hands he unlocked the trunk and wrenched it open. On the floor was a bulky, black bag, and from inside came the ringing tone of a phone call. His heart pounding, he poked at the black plastic with his finger, and inside something seemed to move, something flaccid and heavy. Tearing at the fastenings he ripped an opening in the thick plastic, plunged his hand inside, hardly daring to breathe, and felt the cold flesh of a body. He wrenched open the rest of the bag, and found inside the carcass of a dead pig, the mobile phone strapped to its greasy stomach.

Sweat poured down his face and back, and the huge relief made him tremble and feel faint and sick. But then, as he realised what he'd done, he was swamped by absolute terror. He looked around and seeing no one began trying to re-fasten the plastic bag, grabbing feverishly at the openings with fumbling fingers. It seemed to take an age, but at last it was done and half dragging, half-carrying the heavy bundle to the bank he pushed it into the water. To his horror it floated at first, but then slowly turned over and sank out of sight.

When he returned to the driver's seat he mopped his forehead, and lay back in the seat, gasping for air. After a while he felt a little better, and looked around. All was still and silent. He started the car, turned it round and drove slowly back along the way he'd come. When he reached the top of the hill, he pulled over and took a deep breath. Surely no one would know that he'd looked inside the bag, and if he was questioned about the job he just say he'd carried out his orders to the letter.

He drove on with a sick feeling in the pit of his stomach that it wasn't going to be as easy as he thought. As he began descending to the valley, he saw a black car parked where the railway bisected the dirt road. He pulled over to the side of the track with a crunch of gravel and sat very still. He wanted his dad and Billy. He wanted to go home. He wanted to go anywhere but home. But above all else he wanted another chance. He'd do anything for that.

Right now there was nothing for it but to go and face whatever was waiting for him. Slowly he drove down to the valley floor and drew up next to the car. The man who'd seen him off, so long before, looked across to him, from the driver's seat, got out of the car and walked over. "It's your lucky day, kid," he said, "got another consignment for you, same as before. You don't get a break like that every day." He gestured towards the other car, "Take that auto, the bag's in the trunk."

Luigi, stunned with shocked delight, walked with the man round to the car, settled into the driving seat, and looked up at the impassive face. He could have kissed him, and started dancing with joy, singing the praises of Mr Scaratti for his kindness and understanding.

"Just one other thing, kid," said the man, reaching into his pocket and producing a piece of paper on which was written a name and a telephone number. "I nearly forgot, you gotta ring this mobile just before you dump the goods." Luigi didn't recognise the number, but underneath the figures there was a name: it was 'Billy Barrati'.

The Spider

hance encounters, misheard words and even fleeting glances – life's full of them. They seem trivial enough at the time, but some may affect a person's life, for the rest of their days. Take an unexpected meeting with a giant spider. My friend loathed them when she was young, and the thought of the largest she ever encountered has never left her. So fearsome was that sight that it made her seek sanctuary from danger, and that saved her life. And as she saw it, that was a debt to be repaid, and the only way of doing that, she reasoned, was by living life as fully as she could.

I've only known her when she was well past her prime, but I never think of her as an old lady, although I'm sure her birth certificate would surprise me. She lost her partner only a year or two back – a former boyfriend she re-met when they were both well into their seventies. He was as crazy as her, and they had a whale of a time. She still remembers, more or less, how to play bridge, and until recently drank wine copiously. All her life she conducted a passionate, consummated relationship with the grape, and instead of buying shares or investing in a building society for her old age, she laid down first-growth wines from fabulous vintages. They are all gone now, but I doubt if they all ended up at auction.

Even in old age her zest for life and stamina is astonishing. On a whim we once played bridge all night with her, and rang next day to see if she was tired, only to find that she was on her way to a barn dance. Her powers of recovery never left her – after a champagne-fuelled lunch, whilst looking for her door key, she plunged headlong into the shrubs by her front door, and then went on to play bridge all afternoon. Not long after that she fell downstairs and, worried that she might have harmed her mind, was accepted by, and joined, Mensa.

Fate seemed to decree that even when she did quite ordinary things she often ended up in strange situations. Once, when living in St John's Wood, she answered an advertisement offering a piano for sale. The vendor lived in Hertfordshire, and when my friend saw it, the instrument appeared more antique than operational. The owner, a fierce old lady who'd been on the stage, enquired whether she wished to buy it for profit or pleasure. When she said she wanted it to play, the lady demanded a demonstration, and when it was over it was clear she'd failed the test. Nevertheless she was offered coffee and, as they sat and chatted, they discovered that my friend lived in the house originally occupied by the old lady's piano teacher, and from where the instrument had come. They both felt it was a sign that it should be returned it to its original home, and so my friend bought the piano, and has it to this day. But I've never heard her play.

I've always been interested in first-hand accounts of the Blitz, and she painted for me a vivid image of the bleakness of war for civilians. As a young girl living in London, she was terrified of being killed in an air raid, a very real fear, well grounded in reality. Like many others, she hated the noise of the guns, the falling bombs and loathed the sheer waste and pain of war.

Sleep was difficult for her at the best of times, and she found it impossible during and after raids. She was left exhausted and drained, developed asthma and an eye condition that remained with her for the rest of her life. As time went on she found the raids unendurable and when one was imminent, rather than face a jam-packed public shelter, she crept away to be alone in her parents' flat. One night when a heavy attack was expected she let herself in, and went upstairs to the spare bedroom, where a light bedspread covered the bed.

Moving across the room to pull the curtains, she was struck by how even the bright moonlit was eclipsed by the harsh glare of the circling searchlights, and then something caught her eye. On the middle of the white bedspread, silent and unmoving, was the biggest, blackest spider she'd ever seen. Time stopped, her limbs froze and she gasped for breath. At last, tearing her eyes away from the sinister shape, she fled, and never again entered the room alone. Her fear of bombs was as nothing compared to her terror of spiders, and therefore she always sought safety from air raids in shelters, never again at home. That was lucky for her for, not long afterwards, the flat received a direct hit from a bomb, and was instantly demolished.

Down all the years a dream recurs of that bright night so long ago. She's frozen in the room, and the spider's on the bed, still and silent as the grave. But now it's her familiar – she's learned to love the hated thing that saved her life. She's serviced the debt she owed it through living life as fully as she could, and feels the final payment's getting near. And now she fears that when she dreams one night she'll find it gone, and then she'll have to meet what comes without its help, and make the unknown journey all alone.

The Passenger

I get sick and tired of giving people advice which they just ignore, and sometimes they don't even pay attention when you're trying your best to put them right. And it makes my blood boil the way they think you don't notice them sneaking a look at their watch, hiding a yawn or just turning off when you're speaking. Damned rude! If you go to the trouble of helping others, the least they can do is *listen*, and then do what you say.

In the evening, for example, if you're commuting from London to Reading, I tell them to always get the 6.45 or a later train from Paddington, because passengers thin out after Slough. Experience tempered by common sense! You can tell people things like that until you're blue in the face, and they still think they know better! They'll whinge on about kids and bedtime, 'me time' and other drivel like that, and then have the nerve to complain about the rail service! Women most of them. In my opinion they should be at home looking after the kids in the first place, and not cluttering up offices and getting in the way of real workers doing important things. Not to mention getting promoted over the heads of experienced people because of some nasty little affair they're probably having with the boss. Don't get me on that!

I don't like crowded trains any more than they do, and having to stand is intolerable when you think how much you're paying for the privilege. The difference is that I *do* something about it, and don't just moan. Of course these youngsters are the 'entitled' generation, and you can keep them, as far as I'm concerned. Quite apart from their awful clothes and dreadful accents, they're bloody rude when they're lucky enough to get advice from people who know a damn sight better than they do. And don't get me started on parents and their nauseous brats.

Anyway, back to the 6.45 train, which always goes from platform thirteen. You've got to be sure of being there on time because it leaves promptly, and I'm always out of the office at 5.15, with plenty of time in hand. You wouldn't believe the fuss people in the office make about trivial things like everyone else leaving at six. I just ignore them. If pressed I say, "I'm in the office at 7.30 in the morning, and where are you then, I'd like to know?" That stumps them.

And it's quite true – I'm the first to arrive in the morning – taking the 6.13 which gets in to Paddington at 6.52 and I'm usually at work by 7.30. Then it's a little brew-up of my special English breakfast tea, a thorough glance at the paper I can usually pick up from a seat on the train, and maybe a little snooze. If there's time, that is, before the others come and spoil it all.

The other day a new junior was grumbling on and on about always being the one who brought in the fresh milk every day for our tea. As if it cost her a fortune! "I hope you don't expect me to get it," I told her. "Learn to display a bit more respect for your senior colleagues." It was a useful exchange, and a heaven-sent opportunity for me to address the problem of her body odour. Everyone knew about it, of course, but as usual it was down to me to grasp the nettle! Heavens knows why, but she just burst into tears, and now I have to borrow milk from the caretaker every morning! Some people!

From Paddington to the office it's only six stops on the Tube, but every first Tuesday in the month I'll take a number fifteen bus, because I'm not one of those idiots who's a slave to habit. Not like this old boy in the office, who I've known for years – he's called Tom… Barnes or Barnet, something like that, not that it matters. I noticed that he always had the same things for lunch – salmon paste on white, crusts cut off, an apple and two digestive biscuits, all wrapped in old greaseproof paper. He always left half a sandwich, which he stuffed into his briefcase. I asked him why he did that, and he said it was in case he felt peckish going home on the train. But he added that he never did, and always threw away the half-eaten sandwich! "Fred, get a life," I said. Someone once said that to me. To me! Imagine!

It's important for me to have the same seat on the early train, as I'm prone to motion sickness, and can only travel facing the way the train's going. I've had a lot of abuse when I've simply asked someone to change places. I consider I'm polite, but for some reason they object when I tell them to take those infernal plugs out of their ears when I'm talking to them. Anyhow, I usually get my seat and I'll settle in and put the empty army rucksack on the seat next to me. That usually does the trick of keeping people away, but anyone who tries to intrude on my space gets the steely eye treatment. I can't stop them sitting there, but I'll make them feel uncomfortable, which serves them right. My seat's in one of the single rows, and that means I don't get some idiot opposite, with nothing better to do than stare at my hairpiece, which people seem to find amusing. Also in rows like these, there's no room for yobs to put their filthy feet on the seat, and you don't have to talk to anyone or ever meet anyone's eye.

I look out of the window a lot, and make a note of what I see in the reporter's notebook I carry everywhere with me. I call it my 'Incident Book' and I've kept every one I've ever used. Goodness knows how many hundreds I've got. They're in my bedroom, under the stairs, in cupboards and in the garage, not to mention the shed!

When I was coming home, last night, something annoying happened. On Thursdays I go to a club near Leicester Square for gents who, like me, choose to keep themselves to themselves, when they're enjoying their leisure, and I got to the tube station at 11.34. The train soon came in, and when I'd got a seat for the disabled, as usual, I started to read the adverts. I like scanning them – counting the number of vowels in each advert, and recording the result. I must have collected tens of thousands of them over the years, and one day I'll analyse the data, if I ever get a moment.

I don't often notice other passengers, but the old gentleman opposite caught my eye, because he was unlike the usual riff-raff you get thronging London streets. He was smartly dressed in a three-piece white suit, with a formal necktie and very highly polished brown shoes. Rather central European looking, I thought, with these half-moon glasses and pink cheeks, framed by a neat goatee beard. He had with him a small, neat gift-wrapped parcel.

When the train stopped at the next station a dishevelled drunk stumbled into our carriage, and began walking unsteadily down the carriage peering at each passenger as he lurched past. No one moved a muscle and no one looked up, except the old man. "Don't you screw me, you fucking old Jew," the man shouted, grabbing his lapels and throwing him sideways onto the floor. The old man gave a cry, and when he struggled to rise, the thug kicked him hard in the stomach and began punching him. By the time we were coming into Paddington the couple were rolling around on the floor.

"It's disgusting," said this fat, foreign woman next to me, "grown men, fighting like that." I nodded, and squeezed past them to get to the door, which had just opened. As I did so my shoe crunched on something, and looking down I saw I'd trodden on the old man's glasses. Just my luck! My shoes aren't meant to take punishment like that!

Luckily the Paddington train arrived and left on time, and after Slough I was alone in the carriage. Because of the event on the Tube I'd missed making my usual written entry on the adverts, and so I spent some time examining my shoes for glass shards. Luckily none had penetrated the holes that let in so much water when the pavements are wet, but the amount of chewing gum I had to pull off the soles! Then I relaxed by recording the number of missing platform lights at the stations we passed through.

When I got home, it occurred to me that I should make an entry in the 'Master Incident Book', about my adventure on the underground. I never usually do anything like that without discussing it with my wife, but it was too late to go down to the cellar. If you're tired, it's not pleasant moving about in the dark, and I'd only feel guilty going down there because I think the damp's getting to my old railway timetables. There's a nasty smell like mildew down there, and I wouldn't be at all surprised if the rats aren't back. Sometimes in bed before I go to sleep I feel really panicky about the state the guides will be in when I bring them up to be re-classified. Obviously, Ethel can't do much to help, not in her condition.

When I realised that I'd need to create a new section in the Master Incident Book in which to locate the entry, I just couldn't decide what to call it. I sat in front of the kitchen table, thinking and thinking, but then I realised it was getting really late. So I closed the book, went to bed and fell fast asleep.

Getting Up, Getting On

Marcus Cox looked up from the *Fundamentals of Western Philosophy*, with a wry smile, which reflected mild self-disgust rather than amusement. In the first place he couldn't recall why he was referring to the book, and in the second, although it was an old friend and very familiar, he hadn't done more than dip into it more than a few dozen times in forty years, like so many other books on his shelves. And now, of course, it was easier to check out something using the computer.

His 'library' consisted of the relatively few books he'd read and re-read over the years, and a much larger collection of those he had once intended to read one day. How he'd ached to have the time to digest them when he was working and there was no time; but now he'd got plenty he still didn't read very much. At least he had no more delusions about getting to grips with French, reading all of Tolstoy, Trollope and Joyce, digesting *Seven Systems of Indian Philosophy*, studying the *Koran* or becoming familiar with Shakespeare's complete works.

He sighed but just as he was putting down the book, his eye was caught by a passage, quoting Socrates as remarking that the unexamined life was not worth living. That depressed him, for he'd reached the age when, if he didn't look out, he'd be spending more time living in the past than he had when he was actually in it. "If you know what I mean," he said to an invisible audience, and then checked himself. His wife considered his habit of speaking what he thought to be a sign of premature senility and undesirable. Probably because it reminded her she was getting on a bit as well.

But surely dwelling too much on the past could generate a lot of negative thoughts about one's own life? Soon after he'd retired he'd been through an intense recrimination phase about his failings, and he didn't want that again. Was he young to have gone through that? An older friend of his had reached eighty before he went through a similar experience. His life hadn't been blameless, he'd needed reassurance about the inevitability of human error and Marcus had obliged, giving the old boy comfort. But by the time his friend was eighty-six he'd ceased to worry about such things, for all his attention was taken up with the simple act of living, which by then, was not simple at all.

He put the book back on the shelf, lining it up precisely with its fellows, noticing, with dismay and boredom the dust on the top of the row of books. He sat down, leaned back in his chair and thought some more about life. Winter afternoons in London like this often encouraged him to have dismal thoughts of mortality, and now, for some reason, he felt the urge to revisit his childhood more vividly than before, and see if he could remember things of long ago. But how to do it? Then he had an idea.

When he was about eleven he'd had a serious fever which lasted long enough to keep him away from school for a whole term. He assumed that he was dangerously ill, although his sister told him later that she'd forgotten all about it. Imagine that! Your little brother, near to death for nigh on three months, and you can't recall a thing about it. But he didn't want to think about the illness itself, but thought he might access his past by reliving his experience of getting up after he felt better, and describing the sensory impressions he experienced at the time.

"I suppose we all know what it's like when we're warm in bed and feeling better, but don't yet fancy facing the cold, hard world," he said, speaking to his invisible audience. That provoked an acute recall of an afternoon, long ago, when he'd slipped out of bed, into the deep quiet of the house, for the first time in months. What an illicit feeling that must have given him! Marcus had been reliant on others all his life up to then, and this was his first independent action in an adult world! How he must have wanted to get on with life, and join in whatever was going on! He'd always loathed being excluded from activities, but until now never really appreciated the intensity of his feelings. That was worth knowing, even at this late stage in his life, and he felt excited but apprehensive at the powerful feelings that were emerging from what he was thinking.

In getting up, the first of his senses to be engaged would be touch. Bare feet, richly endowed with nerves, on a cold floor, would be the torch-bearers of sensation, and herald the terrible transition from the warm womb of the bed to the raw reality of life. Holiday memories would surge up – of stumbling from an icy sea across a frigid, gritty beach, over razor-sharp rocks, corpse-white feet puckered and chilled to the bone.

Marcus felt, for the first time, that touch was the sense humans most took for granted. Blind and deaf people are easy to spot, but what of those whose sense of touch is impaired? Are there such unfortunates, and if so, what an impoverished life they must lead! For touch can be the most tender of senses, and we use it instinctively when words fail us. Do we not embrace each other in moments of great emotion as a mother will clasp a baby to soothe and comfort it? Marcus remembered being literally speechless with someone whose mother had just that moment died, and hugging and holding her tight, until the first shock was over. A purely instinctive reaction? He'd never know.

Perhaps the next sense to come into play was that of hearing. Thinking back, he was quite sure that there was a deep, almost dead, silence about the house, when he left the bedroom. And now he wondered why he'd not valued quiet more in his life, and sought out the solace that silence brings. Then he knew why – it was this 'getting involved' business. He pictured himself standing on the landing, listening intently, and gazing out of the window with unseeing eyes, hearing the bustle and clatter of life, getting nearer and clearer, as his ears became acclimatised. And being aware of all the things that had started and were going on without him – family and friends, tradesmen and travellers, all busy with their lives, going about in a world he hadn't inhabited. The very idea! A new and terrible one, and it must have taken some of swallowing.

Surely he must have looked around him now, and sight was next – the all-embracing sense. It was the very end of spring, he recalled, but no bright sun to bring out the fresh green of the garden, just dull English clouds over dull English roofs. Drab, dingy, workaday world! Is this all he'd been waiting for? And might it help explain why all his life he'd preferred the journey to reaching the destination. He remembered how he'd always loved Tennyson's poem 'Ulysses', with its yearning for a lost past, and a longing to marshal what remained of former strength. 'Over the hills and far away' had always appealed to him as a boy, and he'd always travelled widely. And now into his mind burst the idea of how pictures had always appealed to him.

From his very young days he'd known and devoured a three-volume folio set of wonderful prints. Biased towards British art, and naive in its choice of works, he'd found it beautiful. What a gift for a child to know and love good paintings from an early age, for then you own them all your life. His mind flew back to the sight of them. Some he hated: the beetle-black gloom of Velazquez and Rembrandt, Byrne-Jones's aubergine-tinted Pre-Raphaelite palette and the angry, ochre tones of Turner's *Fighting Temeraire*. But his soul sang with the light blues and yellows of Reynolds, the visions of space and light in Furse's *Diana of the Uplands*, Somerscales' *Off Valparaiso*, and the warmth of Singer

Sargent's *Carnation, Lily, Lily, Rose*. And how he loved the precise detail in the narrative paintings of earnest Victorians!

He wondered next what he might have smelt when he came downstairs, for smell and its twin 'taste', are powerfully evocative, and a mere trace can rekindle past memories like nothing else. "Strange how potent cheap music is," says Noel Coward, through the mouth of a character in *Private Lives*, and homely smells and basic tastes work, too. Marcus recalled the aroma inside a pre-war Morris Eight in a vintage car rally he'd once visited, and being flooded with memories of outings with his uncle and sister in a similar car in the 1950s. When they sang wartime songs together because that was when time stopped for Uncle, who'd served in the Middle East, when they looked out for the church that disappeared behind a hill as they drove past, and when AA men saluted members' cars. A lost world, complete and real, conjured up from a whiff of engine oil, hot leather and ancient plastic.

He wondered too, if he smelt the cakes his mother would have been cooking when he wandered into the kitchen. She would have been there, for she would never have left him ill and alone in the house. How would he react to the taste of one of her oven-warm cakes to eat now? The madeleine dipped in tea, reminded Proust of his childhood, and released thoughts that led to seven volumes of dense reminiscences. Perhaps we all have that in us, if we can release the child in us long enough. "Mother's in the kitchen, all's well with the world," I once heard said. But kitchens last longer than mothers, and without them the world is never entirely complete.

Marcus stretched and yawned, stood up and drew the curtains. Then he sat down and considered the journey into his long-vanished past, now less with a knee-jerk regret than a more considered resignation. *How much of our lives are limited by and played out through the senses*, he thought, *and what creatures of emotion and imagination we often are*. Where had he heard that last bit? As for loss, he reflected that Buddha started his own spiritual journey by recognising that change in life was fundamental, and everything disappears or is transformed, including ourselves.

We all lose people and the things we've loved or loathed, while morals, manners, tastes and troubles have their day and fade away. But for us, sometimes the thought of something we've lost catches us unawares, with a visceral sharpness, strengthening with every turn of time's wheel. And the world we once took for granted, and possessed, becomes another's oyster, more alien by the day. He began to sense the first faint yearnings to leave this life and move on. A morbid feeling? Far from it, for the seed carried within it was a true acceptance of natural order and rightness.

Marcus sighed and stood up. In half an hour he felt his mind had travelled immense distances, and none at all. Was that what Eliot meant when he wrote: "And the end of all our exploring, Will be to arrive where we started, And know the place for the first time"? He'd think about that tomorrow – now it was time for a glass of wine. And then, maybe another.

The Caretaker

They may be selling software, driving school buses or preaching sermons, but you can always spot 'naturals' from the moment you meet them. Take me, for example, I'm a natural caretaker, it's what I'm meant to be. And when I'm alone in my building after the office workers have gone, I'm in my seventh heaven.

From my cubby hole just off the main entrance I see it all. The rush and bustle, the gossip by the water dispenser, the late lunchers and the smokers, latter day lepers, having a furtive drag on the steps outside. Then suddenly it's over, and the building's still and calm. Not *clean*, though, not yet – not until my girls have finished. And when they've gone there's the space and the silence, deep and satisfying, the sort that gives you time to ponder on things and get a sense of perspective on life.

Don't get me wrong, though, I don't despise office workers. Just getting to work is a pain for most of them, and often it's no fun when they do get there. That's a shame – especially if there's nothing for them to look forward to when they're not there. All that struggle in life to get either where they don't want to be, or don't really care to be. At least it makes them too busy to think, and that keeps the awful gremlins at bay. The dam that bursts when they retire, and the big thoughts of loss and death, loneliness and liability come pouring in. The curse of freedom, when all you've got left is plenty of time to wonder what's been the *point* of it all.

But it's not just being able to think in the quiet that I love about the job. I walk around the empty offices when the cleaners have done, and it smells fresh and ready for another tomorrow. I've never lost that love of a clean room in the early morning ever since I was at primary school.

Our head teacher was large but not fat, kind but not soft, and we got on like a house on fire. She used to let pupils clean her office in the morning if they'd been good – little ten-year-olds being rewarded by being allowed to do some cleaning! Just think of that. And I got to do more of that than anyone else, don't ask me why. Perhaps because I was reliable, organised and cared about doing it well. Now, even though I'm a grown-up caretaker I'm basically just the same, and it's stood me in good stead.

'Caretaker' is an interesting word, if you stop to think about it. It could mean someone who takes care over what they do; or someone who takes away others' cares; or someone who makes sure that everything is taken care of. Take your pick, because whatever people may think about caretaking as a lowly occupation, all these meanings imply useful, honourable work.

So what helps you do justice to a vocation like that? For a start it helps to keep your eyes open, *observe* what's been going on around you, get to know the layout of every room in your property, the configuration of the furniture and the orderliness (or lack of it) around you. That way you learn something of the people who work there, and the way things are going. There are clues everywhere if you know where to look, and it's not just noticeboards that help you see what's happening. I can spot a company going downhill long before the workers or the even the board had an inkling. It's all there, from the state of the lavatories to the dog-eared 'vision' statements from management in the conference room. And don't neglect wastepaper bins, they can be a treasure trove of information!

In my time as a caretaker I've left some companies just before they went under, or sometimes when they'd still got some time to go. I admit I've used the knowledge to play the stock market, but never as an insider dealer. I've never pried into anything confidential or used share information that wasn't in the 'public domain'. What a lovely, pompous expression that is! How I delight in the English language!

I've always loved words and learning. I went to night school when I was young, and didn't go out with girls or socialise. I wanted to study English literature, but I knew that bookkeeping and accountancy were what counted, and grew to like them and do well. But we were poor at home and I needed to work nights and couldn't study for long. Then I was called up for National Service. Most youngsters hated the discipline of the army, but I didn't. I was naturally tidy and polite – but that didn't mean I was soft, for I could be handy with my fists. In no time I found myself a sergeant, and then I was offered the chance to be selected for officer training. They may have been hard-up for men, but that didn't mean they'd take anybody.

I ended up a captain and acting major, in the Catering Corps, would you believe? Not very gung-ho, but more essential than many who were. I was even offered a regular commission. It was being practical, you see, working hard, listening to what I was told to do, and finding I had a talent for getting the best out of my men. But I turned it down, because I wanted to have more time to think.

In Civvy Street I got a job with a local firm of house removers, doing their books and managing their office. It was a family firm and the boss was getting on a bit. To be honest, his son, Ronald, was a wastrel: Conservative club and playing golf about summed him up, so Molly, the daughter and I did most of the graft, with Teddy, her younger brother. She was pretty and kind, and sweet on me, and I must say I toyed more than once with the idea of taking up with her. But it wouldn't have been fair, because I would never have known if it was her or the business that I wanted. So I left the firm and became a private investigator.

Anyone could set up doing pretty well anything in those days. I chose that line of work because all the things I'd done

– the studying, the army, running an office and above all giving myself time to think – had left me with a good memory and well-honed powers of observation. It's a business, you know, where word of mouth is vital, and I was always efficient and honest, and I did well.

One day a young detective police constable came round from the local nick, for I'd been working on a case that involved them, and they wanted my help. I assumed they'd told him to find out more about me.

"You been in the army?" he started off, and when I told him I was in the Catering Corps, he asked me to make him a sandwich. "Seriously, what did you do there, mate?" he said.

"I was in the Divisional Provisions Depot, at Caterham."

"You a cook, or something?" he says, yawning. So I showed him the photo I'd got in my desk drawer of me with my group. Sixty-eight of us, and I'm in the middle.

"Very interesting – where are you, Leslie?" he says, tossing the photo onto the desk.

"I'm the officer bloke in the middle," I said, "and sit up straight when you speak to me, sonny."

"Sorry about the sandwich crack, sir," he says, hastily. "I won't keep you a moment." It's the only time I ever pulled rank on anyone, but he got under my skin.

I did well for ten years, employed some good men, and several of them have done really well since. But I got bored and anyway, I'd been getting more interested in the stock market for some years. It all seemed fairly straightforward to me, and my investments did well. To tell you the truth I didn't know what to do with the money except reinvest it, and then, of course, I did even better.

I met Susan at an Open University summer school, for I'd never lost my love of getting my head down and studying a bit. I'd always loved films and acting, since I was a boy, so I signed up for a degree course, and one thing led to another and almost before I knew it, I'd got a Masters in Modern Drama, and my tutor had persuaded me to go for a PhD. In no time at all I was beavering away, using my gains in the market to keep me going. What my old mum would have made of seeing me wearing a red gown and a floppy hat at my graduation makes me chuckle. They wanted me to stay on and teach at the university after that, but I was hankering to get back to caretaking, and I had to turn them down.

Susan brought some polish into my life. A lot younger than me, she'd been privately educated in Sussex and Paris, and after an early disastrous marriage had taken up interior design. When we met she was running a thriving business. We went to the theatre a couple of times, got on well, and one evening I asked her back to my basement flat in Pimlico for coffee. She took one look at the place and gasped with horror. "Leslie, you've got to get out of here," she said. "Don't worry, I'll arrange everything." She seemed more turned on about that than any other aspects of our relationship, which suited me fine. And then she realised that she knew nothing about my means. "Darling, Leslie," she said, "it would be lovely to help you move, but it can be very expensive."

To be honest, what with the private detective consultancy in which I'd kept a controlling interest, and the stock market speculation, and being so busy studying, I didn't know how much I was worth, and only knew I didn't spend much on living. So I worked it out, and when I told her what I could afford, Susan was shocked. "My dear man, I'd no idea," she said. "You could buy a large flat in Cheyne Walk for that." So I did, and she was very helpful in moving me in. But she wanted more out of our friendship than I did, and when I broke it off she was so upset. And I was sorry about it too, because I really liked her. But I needed space and time to think about things.

It doesn't take long to tell the rest. Now I live on my own, overlooking the river, with a cordon bleu cook-housekeeper, and a walk-in wardrobe full of Savile Row clothes. I like nice things made by people who know what they're doing, and *care* about getting things right. But I only wear them at home, when I'm on my own, and I'm not there much because of my vocation.

Essentially I'm a natural, professional caretaker, and as I hope I've made clear, it takes time to get it right. No one knows I own a controlling interest in the company that leases the building where I work, or the freehold of the building itself, for that matter. It would be that young detective all over again if they did: "Yes, sir. No, sir. Three bags full, sir."

Why do I go on doing the job? You'll think it's so I can keep an eye on the business, but it's more because it gives me time to think. And make sure that my office staff, for that's how I see them, get that lovely, clean, early morning feeling when they come in for another day at the office, just like the kids in my primary school after I'd cleaned up there. It's the least I can do, seeing as they're keeping the investment profits rolling in for their caretaker, who always has a ready smile and a sincere greeting for everyone. I like to think that when they get depressed about life, they feel happier thinking: "If he can keep cheerful, in such a lousy, badly paid job, with no prospects, then so can I!"

Well, now you know. So why not spare a glance for the people you meet who delight you and others with their work, or the service they give you? These are the winners in life, and if you look hard enough, some of it might rub off on you. And if it does then you can pass it on to someone else. Like I have to you!

THE KITE AND
THE CLOUDS

When I was ten my brother Jim was thirteen, but although
we grew up together, we were never close. That was largely
because I was easy going and dreamy, and he was insanely
competitive, always forcing me to engage in his favourite
activities, with little consideration for the difference in our age.
And so I ran races which I hated, climbed trees, sick with fear, and
played at 'explorers' where I fell over tree roots and into streams,
gashed my knees, and often went home crying. When all I really
wanted to do was read, draw and watch birds. Was that so bad?

Jim would call me a cry-baby, but that didn't stop him forcing
me to compete the next day and, of course, he always won. Once,
though, when he said he wasn't feeling well, I nearly beat him
running. He refused to speak to me for the rest of the day, and
when we played cricket to make up, and I bowled him out, he hit
me on the head with his bat.

We grew up in a cottage surrounded on three sides by woods,
in which hidden paths were crossed by little streams that dried
up in summer; whilst behind the house a grassy meadow rose
abruptly to form a hill. In summer white butterflies would flutter
through the flower-scented air, and high above, a ring of beech

trees was outlined sharply against the sky. I would lie halfway up the slope, in the long grass, busy with insects, and watch the white clouds moving silently across the blue sky, slowly changing shape, imagining the mystical, faery lands where they were bound.

I must have felt, as children do, that life would go on in the same way for ever. But, unknown to me at the time, it began to change, when I was lying in the meadow one day, squinting into the sun, trying to spot a lark fluttering above me. Jim was near the top of the hill, and was yelling to me to join him. I knew there'd be no peace until I did, and so with a sigh, I took one lingering look for my lark, and slouched up the hill to see what he wanted.

"Race you round the three trees," he said, and my heart sank, for this was a run I could hardly manage, let alone win. The three trees were tall old pines, planted along the treeline about a quarter of a mile apart. The race always started from halfway up the hill, and included scrambling over stiles, climbing through barbed wire, dashing along a ditch full of nettles and crossing a stream large enough to have water all the year round. Jim would give me a carefully calculated start ensuring that he'd beat me by a country mile, whooping with delight when he caught up and passed me.

When I reached him this time, he took me by surprise by shouting, "Ready, steady, go!" and pushing me off, to race away in my airtex shirt, khaki shorts and sandals. Usually I never looked back until I'd laboured up the first hill, and reached the stile by the first pine, winded and panting. I would clamber over, look back and see Jim coming up the hill in hot pursuit, but before I'd reached halfway to the second tree he'd have drawn level with me, and was surging past. However, this time I didn't seem to be as much out of breath as usual, and he was further behind me than ever before. Normally he'd be sprawled out on the ground, calm and cool, smiling to see me arrive so far behind him, and I'd be gasping for breath. In fact, he didn't reach and pass me until we were on the third leg, coming up to the last pine.

"You won, as usual," I said, flopping down beside him, delighted with my performance, "but not by that much."

"Must have given you a longer start than usual," he said, sourly, turning on his stomach to look up at the clouds. "Anyway I'm not racing with you again, you're just a kid. I'm only going to run with big boys."

I felt like crying, but then I saw that his face was very white and he was trembling. "What's the matter?" I said. "Have you been stung by a bee or an adder?"

"I'm just a bit dizzy," he said, with a panicky note in his voice. "You'll have to help me get home."

"I can't, I'm too small – I'll go and get Daddy."

"No, no, just stay with me, and hold my hand," he said. "I'll be fine in a moment."

And so the first big change in my little life started with me, aged ten, holding my big brother's hand. After a while, I got bored and began to twist and turn in his grip, and Jim snapped, "Stop doing that," jerking my hand so hard that it hurt. Then he stood up and said, "Come on – race you home! And don't tell anyone what happened."

I said nothing, and life went on much the same. Or so I thought, but things were changing. For one thing I was beginning to shoot up, and the pencil marks Daddy drew on the kitchen wall, when he measured our heights, showed I'd put on several inches in the previous six months, whereas Jim had hardly grown at all. And I vaguely noticed that he didn't run around so much or climb trees like he used to. Jim might have been less physically active, but for some reason his persecution of me intensified, and it started with the den.

It was my idea, for now that Jim was spending less time with me I'd got to know a few local youngsters of my own age. I became the junior member of a 'gang'. Such groups need secret headquarters, and we built the den in a hollow beneath a tree in a hedge bordering a field, where the corn grew high and only wild animals ever ventured. We made walls out of broken branches, stripped bare of leaves and layered vertically, filling the spaces between the wood with mud dug up from a pond we found in a forgotten corner of a local farmyard. We invented wattle and daub! We excavated soil from the roots of the tree, and camouflaged the entrance with sheaths of broad-leaved sycamore branches. It was modest and easily overlooked – part of its appeal as a secret hideout but it was important to us. It was our very own creation.

When our den was finished we didn't really know what to do with it. We held pow-wows like Red Indians, but soon ran out of things to talk about. Then we buried the skulls of small animals and dead birds, and forgot all about them. We even lit a small fire in it, but did nothing with it. We hadn't cottoned on to the fact that it was the challenge of construction that was the most exciting part, like getting to the moon was more enthralling than actually being there. Some wanted to keep it as it was or improve it, others wanted to abandon or even destroy it. Interest was waning, and we began learning how different people can be, and how difficult it is to compromise.

I suppose it was because it was my idea in the first place that made me so attached to the place. I loved the feel of the friable earth, dry and crumbly beneath the roots, the sharp, sappy smell given off by snapped green branches, the scent of the hedgerow, and the sight of the waist-high grass waving in the field above the den. Eventually the others drifted off, leaving me alone and I spent long hours there, alone and quietly content, watching animals and birds, learning that if you're still, nature will come to you.

Jim noticed my absence but knew nothing about the den. One day he secretly followed me and found out where it was. The next day I was there listening to larks, tumbling around in the sky, and he came crashing in, with two big kids. They held my arms as he ripped down branches, kicked away the stones around the fire, unearthed and crushed our pathetic little treasures and left the secret entrance gaping wide. I struggled and wriggled and Jim laughed in my face. I knew he wanted me to cry, but I was determined not to, and didn't. When they released me, I ran out of the den and never returned.

Later, at home, when I asked him why he'd done what he did, he shrugged, turned away and said, "It wasn't much of a den, was it?"

"But it was mine," I cried. "It was mine!"

"Well, it's not now, is it?" he said. "Grow up kid, and leave me alone."

When he had the bad fall, he was out shopping with my parents. After that came doctors' visits, worried consultations behind closed doors and then he spent long periods in bed. I used to creep into his darkened room, and gaze at the pale, sleeping face of a big brother who seemed smaller with every visit. One day an ambulance arrived outside the cottage door and cheerful men in white coats lifted Jim onto a stretcher and took him away. Mummy's eyes were red for days, and Daddy was sad and quiet. I was sent away for a while to stay with my aunt, who lived in a big house near Taunton, which pleased me because she was jolly, and I was friendly with the boy next door.

When I came home Jim was back, and there was a wheelchair in the hall. From then on I never saw him in public when he wasn't in that chair. But I know he got out of it when he thought no one was watching. He'd stagger around the kitchen, and sometimes break a cup or leave a mess – anything that I could be blamed for. I didn't really mind – I suppose he'd bullied me for so long that I thought it was just normal behaviour for a big brother. Anyway, now I could read, draw and watch my birds, and not have to race round three trees.

I spent hours in my meadow, watching the birds, wheeling on the up-draughts of air, drawing plants and reading my books. I felt sorry for Jim and tried to interest him in what I did. I even offered to push him outside into the small garden which bordered the field, but he preferred to sit in his chair, in the enclosed veranda, hour after hour, looking up at the moving clouds. Every day his body seemed more twisted and his speaking more laboured, and

Mummy had to spoon-feed him at family mealtimes. And as he got worse, it was only in his room that he ate anything.

His campaign against me intensified. He was still more able than he made out, and he continued using that to his advantage. I had to be wary, for although I now had my own bedroom, I was often outside and he was always inside the house. There was no lock to my room, and I wouldn't have dreamt of asking for one, so when I found that my collection of birds' eggs had been damaged, or my books had pages torn from them, or one of Daddy's razor blades was jammed under the wooden door handle, I said nothing. And I must have realised how unhappy Jim was, for I bought him a kite.

At first it was just a small one, because it was all I could afford from my pocket money, even though I'd saved up for weeks and gone without sweets. I wanted to take him nearer to his beloved clouds, even if only in his mind. It was an inspired gift, and from that day on, Jim would always be holding a kite that Daddy bought him, twisting and turning it as if in flight. In his mind I suppose he was letting the wind carry him aloft, running freely among the clouds with their sun-lined margins. But as time went on and the kites became bigger Jim grew weaker. Sometimes I thought it was only the latest kite that Daddy made for him that kept him going. When it was assembled it was huge and taut, dwarfing his poor shrunken frame, but he would sit for hours, lovingly feeling its powerful fabric, with his failing hands.

One blustery late summer's day, when we were alone in the house, he called out to me. I walked across to his wheelchair, and he looked up at me, his eyes brilliant and intense and said, "I'm going to the top of the hill, and you've got to help me get there."

"Don't be silly," I said. "We'll never get the wheelchair up the hill. Why do you want to go there, anyway?"

"I want to fly my kite." He grasped my arm and leant forwards his tired eyes alight. "No one's ever flown it – and I want to be the first. You've got to help me."

I wouldn't do it for he was far too weak, but I did what I

70

thought was the next best thing, and hauled him in his chair as far up the hill as I could manage. Then I raced down and returned with the great kite, all folded up but still an immense structure of fabric and wood for a small boy. Jim turned his head sideways on the pillow, and said nothing. I pulled and strained at the strings and cross-pieces and at last, it was ready, the huge structure billowing and writhing, as if desperate to fly. I moved Jim's chair round so that he could follow what I was doing and then hauled the kite to the top of the hill, where the sky seemed near enough to touch. Up there the wind was so strong that I could hardly stand up, and the clouds, fleeing away to the east, were being jostled and pushed by the warm west wind, with now and then a splinter of dazzling sunlight seeping out from behind them. I screamed down to Jim to watch as I heaved the kite upright and, held on tightly to the string, but it was snatched from my grasp, and away it whirled, like a great bird.

I ran down to Jim and turned when I reached him, looking, with shaded eyes, to see it, taut and wonderful, riding the sky and moving with the scudding clouds. "Look at it go, Jim!" I shouted, and only then realised what I'd done. For, when I glanced down at him, his body was writhing with hatred, and his face was contorted with rage.

"I'm so, so sorry, Jim. I'll make it up to you, I promise I will!" I cried.

With a great effort he raised himself up, and I bent my head to listen. He grunted and spat into my face and turned away. Wiping my face and looking up, I saw that the kite had almost disappeared, and from that day on, when we were alone, he never spoke to me again.

Meanwhile, in spite of Jim, I enjoyed life as never before. Most of all I loved the creatures I came across and watched in my happy wanderings. I was beside myself with joy when I spotted a crayfish in a local stream and brought it home, feeding and caring for it in a tank I kept in the kitchen before returning it to the wild. But for the moment, and under my care, it was my pride and joy. I showed it to Jim who turned away, quietly mumbling, for my parents were there, and he was careful not to let them see him ignoring me.

It was the crayfish that brought things to a head for us. I'd been out in the field and came into the house to check if Jim needed anything. I found him in the kitchen, leaning over the sink, making horrible, gurgling noises. He only did that if something amused him, or when I got into trouble. Then I saw what he was doing. Somehow he'd boiled up a kettle of water and poured it into a basin. Then he'd speared my crayfish with a fork, and was dipping it into the water, the creature wriggling and writhing each time he hauled it out. There was a smile of pure happiness on his face that chilled my blood, and he was drooling with delight. I threw myself at him, beating him with my fists, and he fell backwards into his chair, tipping the basin and the crayfish onto the floor, and upsetting the boiling water over my arm. I screeched with pain and falling to my knees, grabbed the poor, flayed creature and carried it gently to the sink. Taking a kitchen knife, I stabbed it again and again, until it was a shredded mess of obscene, reddish pulp.

"Why, Jim, why?" I gasped, through the pain of my scalded arm, turning to look him very closely in the face.

"It wasn't much of a lobster was it?" he said, laughing up at me, with his crooked face. "Grow up, kid."

I'd beaten him with my fists in passion, but what I did now was in cold blood. My arm was red and raw but I left it untended, as I boiled another kettle of water, and picked up the basin from the floor. I knelt down, and pulled off the slipper and sock of Jim's left leg, exposing his soft, white twisted foot, and placed it in the basin. He was quiet and unresisting, and I wondered if he knew what was going to happen.

When the water had boiled I picked up the kettle, and carried it over to where he was sitting in his chair, with his leg still where I had left it. I bent down low, to make sure he heard every word, and pushed my face close to his. "This is for the lobster, and all the things you've done to me," I said.

He looked up at me with those bright eyes of his, glowing like embers on a bed of dull-red hatred. And in that instant I knew exactly what he wanted, and what I should do. What he wanted more than pain, more than anything, and what I knew I must not fail to do. And as I poured the boiling water away into the sink, I saw the mocking look die away and the colour leave his eyes, their brilliance turning dull, like those of a dying fish.

Young as I was then, I knew I was right. Somehow I knew that if I'd scalded his foot, he'd have won something important. So, although in great pain, I felt free and light-hearted, and it must have showed, for he lunged forward and spat in my face. But he'd lost and he knew it; lost his last race with me, and lost it for ever. I saw it in his eyes and he saw it in mine.

I cleaned up the kitchen and Jim, and wheeled him back to his room in silence, for now we were far beyond words. I left the house to seek help for my scalded arm and somehow Jim managed to get back to the kitchen, reach into a cupboard, find and then drink a whole bottle of bleach. He must have hurried, for I always suspected it was me he wanted to find him. And what I saw when I did come back I wouldn't have wished on anybody. But I don't brood on what happened, and time often softens things it doesn't heal, although the puckered skin on my arm still reminds me of that terrible scene.

Looking back I think he was a monster, and if I had to write his epitaph, I'd write: "Not much of a life, was it, Jim?" He almost won, you know, for I'm ashamed to say that as he weakened I'd taunt and goad him as he sat in his wheelchair, shouting in his face that I was going out running, and that he'd never catch me now. And when he writhed, spitting venom like a snake and crying out with pain and frustration, I'd shout in his ear, "Who's a cry-baby now?"

I'd like to think that I only treated him badly because of the way he'd treated me, but that I never descended to his level of evil. How he must have wanted that! And I do think he was pure evil, my brother, and not fit to live. Evil begets evil, and he wanted to purge me of every shred of kindness and pity, and join him in the hell of causing pain and hurt to others. And when I denied him that, it was the final straw. So I try not to feel too guilty about leaving the bleach where he could easily reach it, with the child-proof top unscrewed. But if I'm honest, you know, it's still something I don't care to think too much about.

ONE LAST LOOK

I t's thirty years now since Albert died, but I still can't explain why he appears so vividly in my mind's eye whenever I think of him. It's not that I've got exceptional visual recall, or even a decent memory. So why can I conjure up his face, figure and gestures so readily, as plain as day? It's a mystery. More so when I think that I really knew so little about him.

He was fifty-three and I was seventeen when we worked together in the late fifties. By today's standards he would seem very thin, and he stooped badly, as if he'd once been injured. He had a ravaged, deeply etched face beneath a high, hairless brow, but it was his hands you noticed. They were pianist's hands, flexible and fluent, with immense spans, and he played superbly. He'd started life in the pit, somewhere in the north, and someone must have recognised an exceptional musical talent that eventually led to his solo debut at the Wigmore Hall. But then came the war, and his nerves were shattered by German bombs, and he never again played in public. And so he worked in the City of London as a book-keeper for fourteen years.

He was what a gentler age called a 'natural gentleman'. He was kind, modest and considerate; a church-going Christian, but carrying his devotion so lightly in his dealings with the world, that I suspect, few discerned its true depth. One day, perhaps on a trip organised by his church, he came on a trip to the Cotswolds, and swore that he'd return and live in the small town surrounded by steep, wooded valleys where I lived for a time. And come he did, this man of fifty, with his youngish wife and great talent for playing the piano. He got a job in a local music shop that sold vinyl records, sheet music, instruments, and pianos, and it was there we met and worked together. Now, looking back over the years, I believe that we were truly happy for a while.

The shop was owned by a local man formerly the manager of a large music shop in Gloucester, who must have had some musical training, for he played the organ competently at funerals and weddings. He was ambitious, and a member of one or more of the local clubs, like the Chamber of Commerce or the Round Table. These connections were important in a small provincial community in those days, perhaps they still are. He seemed to be a biggish fish in a small local pond, and a lot of business came his way through personal contacts. He had an eye for the ladies, but I don't know if he had affairs with any of our customers, for he never served in the shop. Sometimes his wife popped in. She was sweet and polite, always called me 'Mr' which was music to the ears of a youngster with no confidence, and sometimes she brought their little baby into the shop. That delighted Albert, who showed it such affection and handled it so well, that it made you wonder why he and his wife Joyce, had never had children of their own.

It's well over half a century since we worked together in that shop, ordering records and serving customers. Old Mr Whittaker, the piano tuner, grey-haired and bent, was on the payroll, too. The war had left him with abdominal injuries that doubled him up with pain, and for which he took a powdered solution from an old medicine bottle. But he went on moving pianos, wrenching and heaving at them as if his life depended on it. I used to wonder why he went through the agonies that caused him, and I still do.

Then there was Fred, a bulky, abrupt French polisher of similar vintage to Mr Whittaker, with hands and fingernails the colour of conkers. In his younger days, he'd been a marine who could run all day long, asking only that he could put his feet up for five minutes in any hour. He was proud of that. And there was a lame accountant from round the corner, who did the books, and looked just like a hedgehog, and a dazzling public school youth from a well-off Painswick family, who helped in the shop and swept all before him. Even then, whilst still at school, he played the piano at a London hotel and, after Cambridge, he planned to be a barrister. I admired him more than anyone I have known before or since, and sometimes thought how much I'd like us to meet, now that age, education and experience had diminished the distance between us that existed then. But now, I'm not so sure. I've gone back once too often, enough times not to want to run the risk of another disappointment.

A crazy youth appeared towards the end of my stay in the shop. To him days possessed colours, and he purported to repair clocks. Someone entrusted him with a hefty timepiece that he dissected into a thousand pieces, that I doubt were ever reassembled. He was an untidy boy. There was a curtain behind the counter that hid a staircase where we kept huge piles of cardboard boxes that no one ever moved or tidied. Albert fell over something the lad had left on the stairs and a cascade of Christmas decorations fell on him as he struggled in the dark, before stumbling out into the shop. He made a dazzling entrance, his hair and clothes drenched with the glittering fairy dust we used in the Christmas window display. He was the mildest of men, but as he burst out into the shop, empty boxes tumbling around him, he gave a mighty cry of rage which startled me, and I wondered what he could be like if he was seriously upset. Later, when I asked him, he confessed that he'd once thrown a man who'd annoyed him over a wall when he was in the army.

Our part of the Cotswolds attracted well-heeled creative types like artists, musicians and poets. Two of the many customers I served come to mind. One was a tall, stooping composer, who told me once that he was immensely flattered to be asked by a young researcher if she could write her doctoral thesis on him and his work. I found out later that he was mentored by Delius, whom he'd met in a restaurant, and was regarded as one of the twentieth century's finest songwriters, having put more of Houseman's poems to music than any one else.

Another customer was a well-spoken, heavily built, dishevelled but amiable drunk who used to roll into the shop, reeking of booze after Saturday lunch, and play one of the pianos in the showroom, his stumpy fingers dancing over the keys. "Used to keep wicket for the school," he said to Albert one day.

"Would that be Harrow, sir?" asked my friend.

"If you guessed anything thing else you'd be wrong, old boy," the man laughed, playing with great gusto, whilst puffing away on the cigarette dangling from his lips, below a brown-stained, moustache.

In those far-off days, the long-playing gramophone record, or 'LP', was state of the art, and there were magnificent recordings on prestigious labels like Deutsche Grammophon for less than two pounds. Albert and I would play these, and it gave me an enduring love of music, especially that of Liszt and Schumann. I even gave a talk to a local music appreciation society, illustrating it with recordings.

One day I drove over the hills to Minchinhampton in a Morris Eight delivering LPs narrating the whole of the New Testament to comfort a lady invalid who lived in a large house on the common, hushed into silence by her illness. And I also took a little Dansette record player to a middle-aged spinster teacher that I set up for her in her modest suburban house, politely evading her enquiries about girlfriends. I don't suppose her budget ran to LPs, and pop singles wouldn't have interested her, and so I guess it just gathered dust, and did nothing to help her through the long, solitary hours. I felt sorry for these nice women, each in their own different way, so sad and lonely.

Then, like Christopher Robin, I went away and left part of my childhood behind. Albert died not so long afterwards, and I kept in touch by letter with his wife Joyce until she was eighty-eight, and then came the silence. She thanked me once for keeping in touch 'down the years', which I liked, because I felt Albert would have appreciated my keeping in touch with her. To me it was a way of thanking him for being my friend. But I wonder what he would have made of Joyce in her old age, for to judge from our correspondence, she could be either charmingly eccentric or completely cuckoo.

Not long ago I went back to see the shop for one last look and I found it had ended its days as it had lived. A music shop now only in name, all washed up, silent and empty. The shelves, made of perforated stiffened cardboard, which we used all those years before, were strewn over the floor and the pianos were long gone, along with the glittering saxophones and clarinets. Of course, there was no trace of Albert or Joyce, who had lived above the shop, no Mr Whittaker, bent double in pain, or the French polisher reliving his youth, no limping accountant, or silly boy filleting clocks on purple days, or foolish, flirting owner. No boozy Harrow wicketkeeper, and no composer of sweet English songs. Just me, left with my fading memories, but still with a sharp visual image of a man whose features are the only ones I ever see clearly when I think of another person. Someone I seem to have known closely all my life, without really knowing much about him at all.

THE CHOICE

The Norsemen feared no human foe or anything that lived,
but they knew well that caution's best when nature's at the
helm. Almost as soon as they could walk they'd learned of
winds and waves and keenly sensed their power. And thus they
lived and thrived, when others died.

The year, at first, gave promise to be fair and mild. Late
winter ice, which fringed the sounds with freezing crusts, melted
in good time. The gales that blew in early spring soon spent
themselves, and light winds smoothed the white caps in the bay.
And then, beneath clear sunny skies, the snowy mantle on the
chilly hills came streaming down and made green pastures fit for
flowery May. The late-lit days of summer sun came next, with
gently lapping waves, sea-roaming for the fit, and spoils to share
from war on alien soil. But even as the trees lost leaves dark skies
arrived, now streaked with skeins of birds all southern-bound,
heralding the days that keep men house-bound half the time.
No longer open skies for them above the moving sea, or restless
sleep on foreign shores, beneath a waning moon.

The bitter cold locked in both men and beasts: longship laid
up on oaken beams, swords sheathed and stacked, the children's
clothes all sewn up tight. And in the Mead Hall, *Langhaus* in the
olden days, men ate and drank and argued half the night away.
Mewed-up young men began to chafe, and hot-heads raged
without a lord to cool them down. For he was dead and elders

too – all drowned when home-bound from a feast across the stormy sound.

Four sons were left and only one could rule. Within the clan each man may make his choice and none of them was lord by right. Kin disagree, tempers run high, the fighting starts, and someone nearly dies. When blood is spilt, then feuding's out of hand, and that will split a clan unless it's stopped. The old men who are left, debate at length and in the Mead House give the kin their thoughts.

"There is a wise man we would seek to aid us in this hour," Magnus their spokesman said. "He knows the clan and gave us help before, when others offered none."

"Old man, sure he is long dead now," a younger kinsman sneered.

"No, he lives still we hear, upon a rock-bound coast, sea-leagues away and those across a winter sea." Kinsmen looked down into their drinking horns, and no one said a word.

"So which of you, whose name breeds terror in the heart of foes, will venture on the seas, you warriors of the waves?" old Magnus laughed, "Or will you rest so cosy by the fire, happy to yarn and then sleep safe, all nestled in your beds, so wifely warm? It makes me yearn to lie with our late lord, that I should live to hear you have no voice."

One of the kin spoke up. "You know full well, there's no one here who fears to ride the roughest wave, or face the fiercest gale. But hear my words – our toughest ship's not built to sail in winter's storms. And if this man of yours is dead, what then? And living, might he not just leave us to our fate? For this we'd risk our lives – and drowned, what help are we to those at home?"

Old Magnus sighed. "Without such help, what hope have we? Were we still young by now we'd have the longship out, made ready for the trip and then be off upon the darkened sea. Think on, it grows so very late."

"Why should this sage of yours come to our aid?" another asked.

"Because he is hall-brother to our late dead lord. Who saved his life when they were young – a debt as yet unpaid."

And so the words flew back and forth and that was good, it cooled men down. Then, like the kin, the weather changed: fogs cleared away, seas calmed and rueful men laid plans to seek the sage upon his island home. Out came the longship from its winter's shed, new-tarred and sleek, spare sails well stowed, and fully manned it slid away into the frigid waves. Now those at home could only wait and hope.

★ ★ ★

Two silent weeks went by, but on the third they heard the crunch of pebbles on the beach. The crew made haste to land and laughing with relief lent salt-caked arms to help their guest ashore. Well covered in a cloak of grey he walked along the beach towards the gathered clan, appearing as they'd hoped he would: tall, straight, long-bearded, keenly eyed. The ring of gold he wore upon his hand, the kin knew well, for their dead lord had worn one, too.

The clan he faced were fierce and cruel, but true to death to those who had their trust, and he must win their hearts. "When last I walked with your late lord," he said, "I think that few of you were weaned. Deep ties of blood and debt now bring me here to honour my old friend, and help to keep his clan as one." He paused, and then they cheered, and thus he knew he'd hit the mark.

★ ★ ★

After a week, he'd learned what each man thought and then to honour him and heed his words, a feast took place in the Mead Hall. The eating done and drink at hand, the kin sat crowded round the fire. At last Old Magnus called for quiet and gestured to their guest. The sage stood up and raised his cup and cheers rang through the hall, then silence fell, so men could hear his words.

"Now is the time to choose your lord. There are four heirs, as you well know, but only one may rule. May then I seek their thoughts, and judge the fittest to succeed?" His stock was high within the hall, and gladly they gave leave.

"If you were lord which natural force would serve you best?" he asked the brothers four. "How would you rule and govern such a thing? Now state your case, and if well made, I've powers to reward." The hall grew tense, the sage well knew how well-judged words can tip a balanced scale.

"Air is my choice," thick-bearded Bjorn, the eldest born, replied, straight off. "Not just to breathe, but moving as the wind – a formless foe, well known to all men here. At sea it splits our sails, and breeds boat-breaking waves; on land it unmakes thatch and flattens tidy corn with heavy blows. It howls around my house the whole night long, and gives my children wings of fear to flutter in their dreams." There was a roar from the kin, but Bjorn wasn't done. "All winds I'd temper to my will: I'd steer the Northern Gales away to waste their strength on barren land; East Wind and I would freeze the blood of foes and keep them harmless by their hearth and home. The shy breeze from the south, I'd coax to spread her balmy touch on sleeping babes and mothers all; and when it blows I'd ride astride the rushing Western Wind, that blows our sails towards the rising sun."

"If it were so, the moving air would truly have a Wind Lord to obey," the wise man said, in a dry tone.

"And you?" he said to Leif, next eldest in the line. "What is your choice? Now have your say."

"I cannot match the flurry of those words," answered Leif. "But I would choose the earth, for it is all to me. It guards the seeds that sleep the winter long, and in their season make corn to feed all men. It is the bedrock of my house that keeps all those I love both warm and dry, and when it's time to die I'll sleep in its embrace. This earth I love is wise and strong, more so than me. My hand upon it would be light: I'd seek its aid to make our ploughs dig well, grow healthy crops and build stout homes on stable ground. And help all things live fully and keep well."

"Be not deceived," the sage replied. "Natural things seek little counsel with we humankind, do not confuse a force that helps us feed, with one that cares for man. But you speak kindly and that is pleasing to my ear."

"Speak freely," next he said to lean and thin-faced Brand, third eldest of the four. "Give your claim voice, so all may know your will."

"Fire, fire for me, to forge and form," cried Brand, and in the firelight saw great things take shape. "What melts and moulds can form the very stuff of life: swords, shields and armour, ploughshares, too. Thus by my hand and with my fire I'd fashion things as yet unknown: fine tools and jewels, well forged with flame and flux. And fiery things for warriors too, so all would wonder at my skill."

Both young and old admired his work, but Brand was not liked by the clan. The sage sensed this, and saw the anger in the boy. "Fire's a force, not lightly held in check," he said. "Things forged in heat may take strange shape, when later cooled."

He turned to last born Jon, so quiet and kind. "What thoughts have you to help us in our quest?"

"Water's my choice, for when my work is done, I sit beside the stream and think," said Jon. "It's always there to calm my mind and flushes anger out. It's ours to drink, it cleans and soothes and on its breast we travel to new realms. It falls upon our land and feeds our crops, and so gives life to all. I'd give it freely, so that all might drink and wash out ills."

"To carry out that task," the sage replied, "power more potent than I have ever held is needed. But it was well said, and you have had your say."

The contest's done and now the judgement's due. Bjorn stared round, both fierce and strong, whilst Leif sat calm and still; Brand scowled and Jon smiled, lost in thought. Clamour arose, the cups were filled and wagers flew.

Then silence grew and men looked to the sage.

He paused awhile, to let the tension grow, and then he rose to speak.

"I never heard the like of these good thanes, in giving answer to my quest for fame," he cried. "And power I give to worth, as I first said, but mark this well: much magic is but wisdom 'neath a cloak. Now listen to my judgement on the trial. No one, I think has lost for all spoke well, but only one can win, and Bjorn's is the prize."

He turned to him and let the cheers subside. "The form of your reward, the 'magic', lies in words." Those in the hall who wanted more, looked down, but he had power to end things well. "What each man chose revealed his strength, but over used this weakens and is quickly spent. So Bjorn, Master of the Winds, is leader born, but airborne lords still need a place to land. So with help from Leif he'll need to find firm ground, where dwell strong ties of hearth and home, which families need when oft their menfolk roam." Men were standing now, and cheering.

The sage held up his hand, and said, "A man full-suited to command and lead, though firmly earthed, is still possessed of need. To hold and keep his kin intact, the lord needs things that others prize and lack. And to young Brand, fire-master that he is, he looks for useful things to fashion, forge and trade. And now to Jon, the wisest though the youngest of the four. He is the one to whom his lord should turn to mete out kindly words, stronger than strength of arms, to bring both harmony and heal. And now you have your lord, and he has those to help him, who have strengths he lacks."

The kin knew he had chosen well, but Brand threw down his staff and pushed out of the hall. All saw him go, but none would bid him stay.

★ ★ ★

Next day the sage and Bjorn walked to the shore, to where the longship lay. The sage said his farewells, men manned the oars and then the ship put out to sea.

Men thought that they had foundered, for they never returned. Only a boy on the heights saw things as they were – saw Brand and his cronies put out from the shore, saw a flash and a flare and a glow in the sea. Then the wet fog rolled in from the bay to the sound, and the boy called his dog and turned back to the land.

The last words of the sage to the newly made lord, who was sad at his leaving, went largely unheard. "Do not grieve at our parting, the world carries on, but for comfort, if needed, be sure of one thing – though I've lived like a pauper, I'll die like a king." And that was his passing, out there on the sea – the pyre of a wise man in full majesty.

FALLING IN LOVE

P rovident International moved on from its provincial building society origins long ago, but if it makes business sense, its board members still prefer to embrace a paternal parochialism. Maintaining family affiliations, as long as they are combined with proven ability, still carry weight with the descendants of its founding fathers. The Gilmores are a good example. Charlie, now deceased, the company's chief treasurer for thirty years, joined PI as a humble office boy, and his youngest son Maurice, thirty-eight years old, educated at Westminster, Oxford and Harvard Business School, is now the company's youngest ever group finance director.

Maurice is sitting in a taxi and running late. He glares at his wristwatch for the third time in two minutes, takes a deep breath and pulls some papers from his briefcase. He re-reads the agenda of the meeting he's due to attend with fierce concentration, and finds that one obscure financial appendix contains a minor error. He tuts, shakes his head and makes a neat note in the margin with a slim silver pencil, which he takes from an inside pocket. Then he reaches for his mobile phone, finds that he's left it in his office, curses under his breath, and stuffs the papers back into his briefcase. He drums his bony fingers on his knees, and feels one of his headaches coming on.

It's Friday lunchtime and a clammy summer's day in the City. Maurice is out of sorts, for he seldom leaves his office to waste time talking to others, and when a meeting's unavoidable usually summons them to meet him there. Now the decorators are in, making it impossible for him to work at his desk. Who on earth allowed them to disturb him during working hours? His PA didn't seem to know, and didn't seem to care much either.

He wriggles his lanky frame, shifting his bottom on the hard plastic seat of the old taxi, twisting his seat belt tightly round his chest like a tourniquet. A cold rivulet of sweat makes its way down the middle of his back, and even his silk shirt feels sticky. He notices that there's something brownish on the floor giving off a sweetish smell that makes him want to retch, and mops his brow with a spotless handkerchief. Then he peers through the streaky window at the passing view.

What he sees is depressing. On the pavement, pockmarked with chewing gum, he sees City clerks and building workers smoking, texting and drinking beer from bottles, enjoying being outside a mock Victorian pub. Beside them desiccated shrubs struggle for life in the rock-hard earth of plastic plant-holders, overflowing with pizza cartons and beer-rimmed glasses.

Outside Bank tube station, the taxi, bumping and jerking its way through the fuming traffic, collides with a shaven-headed despatch cyclist who looses off a string of obscene words at the cabbie. He swears back fluently, throwing in a rude gesture for good measure, and after glancing at Maurice in his rear-view mirror, shakes his head with a grin.

Maurice reflects on the adroit way the working classes handle issues like that. He'd lay money that the actors in the little drama wouldn't even remember it ten minutes later, but if it was him he'd fret about it for hours, rehearsing what he might have done, devising how to react in the future, and knowing he'd get it wrong when it came to the test. He's been trained to analyse the past and plan ahead, but it's the present that's his downfall, for he can't respond fast enough, and usually comes off worst. How he hates not being good at things! He's been expensively nurtured to do things well, conditioned not to fail. God, his headache is getting worse. What's the driver muttering about?

"Lower Regent Street. What number, mate?"

Maurice, who hates being called 'mate', snaps out the number and says, "Do you want it in writing?"

"Too much trouble to be civil is it, mate?" asks the cabbie.

"Too civil to be much trouble," he wants to reply, but desists, aware that it would fall on deaf ears. How he longs to be working in the peace and the quiet of his office! Damn those decorators!

The cab jerks to a halt, a little short of his destination, a thick, hairy arm points at the meter, and a long-suffering voice demands payment. He counts out the exact fare using as many coins as possible with no tip, and the cabbie, looking at the change, grunts, and releases the passenger's door. The cab roars away and Maurice, turning back from the road, nearly trips over some bulging plastic bags near the kerb, which the cabbie had spotted but he hadn't. He drops his briefcase.

Removing a sticky wodge of discarded chewing gum from the hand-tooled leather with a grimace, he makes his way to the office for the meeting. Mounting the steps of the Victorian building, he pushes through the heavy revolving door and finds himself in a shabby passageway whose walls are covered with scratched, old-fashioned tiles. After the heat and noise of the street it's pleasantly cool and calm, but the condition of the building appals him, for he's forgotten how many old properties his company has accumulated over the years. He sees a marble counter on the left-hand side of the corridor, and on it a printed notice saying, 'Reception'. He signs his name in the dog-eared visitors' book, noting that no one is on duty, and that the last entry reads: 'Mickey Louse' and 'Donald Fuck'.

The passage is being redecorated and evidence of the painters' lunch and lifestyle is on the floor. On the greasy *Sun* newspaper, open at page three, he sees two empty cigarette packets, one crumpled, the other full of blackened butts, half a greasy bacon butty, three crushed containers of Red Bull and a broken paint roller wrapped in a smeary rag. He assumes the painters are the authors of the entries in the register.

"How can I help you?" says a voice, and Blossom Harris, senior security and reception officer, emerges from the small room behind the counter. Although a few inches short of five feet and inclining towards the spherical in shape, she carries an air of authority in her smart sky-blue uniform festooned with yellow badges. She repeats her question, more loudly this time, for there is a security camera in operation, and she wishes her diligence to be recorded.

"You could have helped me by being on duty in the first place," snaps Maurice. Behind the shades her eyes narrow.

"I'm Mr Gilmore, group finance director," he says, "and I've a meeting with Mr Thompson, the personnel manager. Where can I find him?"

Blossom shuffles some papers on the counter, uneasily. What had he said? Gilmore? She reaches for a list of senior staff on a clipboard, the names garnished with teacup rings and headed: 'Staff List: Display on Board until Further Notice'.

"Room 219, Group Headquarters, Leadenhall Street, EC2," she announces, triumphantly.

"No, no, that's *my* office. Thompson, Thompson," he almost shouts, as he spells out his name.

Blossom is not a trained SSRO for nothing. "Calm down, sir," she says, adding. "Have you been drinking?"

"Of course not," he snarls. "Here, give me that." He grabs for the list of names, but Blossom holds on, grimly.

"That's company confidential," she gasps, between tugs.

"It's the company I work for," he shouts, pulling out from his pocket his identity badge with the photo attached. "Can't you see that? Isn't it plain enough?"

Blossom glances at the card. "You should display that at all times," she says, primly.

Maurice gives a shout of rage, and the painters, just returned from the bookies, listen with polite interest. He wheels round and points at them. "And why do you let people like them write rude things in the visitors' book?"

"Here don't you start accusing people of things they ain't done," says the larger of the painters indignantly. "Anyway, only a bit of 'armless fun. You should lighten up a bit, mate."

Maurice ignores him and, reading the list clasped in Blossom's iron grip upside down, sees that Dr Wayne Thompson, director of human resources, is in room 506, on the fifth floor. "It's there! There! Right in front of you!" he jabs at the name, almost screaming with rage.

Blossom looks at the painters and shrugs, and they grin back. It's Friday and everybody's happy. Except, as usual, Maurice Gilmore, MA, MBA, ACA.

Wearily he turns and walks towards the lift. This ancient cage, wheezing and creaking, has conducted staff up and down six floors for the best part of a century. Inside its safety gate the cabin is lined with faded, cracked veneer, and decades of use have left ugly marks on the walls, whilst the surfaces of the dull, brass fitments are covered in moist, sticky fingerprints. Only the carpet has been recently renewed.

Maurice pulls back the stiff safety gate, opens the inner door and steps into the lift. He's about to push the button for the fifth floor, when the doors are wrenched aside, and Carly King bursts in. She is twenty-four, tall, slim, heavily made-up, and works in the public relations office.

"Which floor do you want?" Maurice asks her abruptly, in a posh voice, his hand poised on the metal control panel.

"Fourth, please," she replies, and he presses the button. The aged structure heaves itself upwards, jerking and rattling, and slowly gathers speed, ascending inside a lift-shaft, encased in wrought-iron filigree and surrounded by chipped and discoloured stairs. When it has nearly reached the fourth floor it gives a slight shudder and stops.

Maurice and Carly, aware of the sudden silence, look at each other for the first time. There's no sign of an emergency bell-push, but Maurice spots a small box on the wall with the words 'telephone' printed on it. He opens the door and finds inside an ancient phone, to which a note had been attached, saying 'Security Awear'. And sure enough, when he lifts the receiver the line is dead.

"Sod it," he shouts, banging the wall with a clenched fist. "I do apologise," he says to Carly. "I'm sure we won't be here long." Under the make-up her face is ashen, and she's breathing quickly. She starts frantically rooting around in her handbag for a tissue, but drops the bag and the contents spill out over the floor. She bends down sobbing softly, and little black rivers course down her cheeks from her moistened eyeliner. Maurice bends down to help, and hands her a snowy white handkerchief from his top pocket.

She accepts it with a mumbled, "Thanks," without looking at him. Rubbing away the tears, she stares at the black smudges on the fine cotton.

"I'm sorry, I've spoilt your lovely handkerchief," she cries, handing it to him. "I'll wash it, and let you have it back, I promise. Tell me where to send it."

"Keep it," he says, thrusting it back.

"It's just that I hate lifts," she cries, renewing her sobs.

"Well, no one actually *likes* them, do they?" he says. "But we have to put up with them." He glances at her, surprised by the lovely features, revealed now the make-up's gone, and can't help noticing the short skirt, and the shapely, bare legs. Usually he sees such things only at a distance and close up, finds them disturbing.

"If it doesn't move soon, I'll use my mobile," he says, forgetting he's left it in his office.

Carly sniffs, "Please tell my boss the lift got stuck, Mr Gilmore. I don't want him to think I'm always late."

"Yes, yes," he says, testily. "How do you know my name?"

"The case you're carrying has a name on it, and I guessed it was yours. I can read, you know."

"Quite right, well done," he replies, and receives a sullen stare. "Why don't we sit down?" he says, noticing the new carpet.

She gives him a quick, suspicious glance, and sensing he's harmless, sits down, demurely curling her legs under her. How gracefully she moves, he thinks, and sits down beside her. It's very hot in the lift, and he fishes the agenda out of his briefcase to use as a fan.

"Do you mind if I take off my jacket?" he asks, after a little while.

"Why should I mind?" she replies, puzzled at such an odd question.

"This is so irritating," he fumes. "I'm already late for a meeting."

"Me too, I was really delayed in the traffic, coming from Oxford Street."

Maurice decides to let that pass, convinced she's been wasting company time on long-lunch shopping. "Have you been with the company long?" he asks.

"Not long," she replies, in a flat, disinterested tone.

"How are you getting on? Do you like it here?"

"I've known worse. They don't expect much from you, so that's what they get."

"Not in my department, I'm glad to say," he replies, curtly.

"Lucky I don't work for you then, isn't it? Anyhow they're good about sick leave."

"What do you mean? Do you need a lot of medical attention?"

"I mean they understand if you sometimes need time off to look after a sick relative. You have to make it up later, of course."

"I disapprove of informal arrangements like that," he snaps, "and I've never taken a single day off sick." It was true enough but, even to him, the words sounded pompous and self-righteous.

"Well, never too late to start, they say. Anyway, what is this, the Spanish Inquisition?"

You see, he thinks, she's got this natural quickness. Why is the world so full of capering cockneys and lippy Liverpudlians? But what did it matter? She was just a nothing. But somehow it did, and he knew that she wasn't.

"What do you plan to do with your next leave?" he asks, as usual getting off to a wobbly start.

When she does take time off, and it isn't that much, Carly spends most of it helping her mother with her handicapped brother, Darren. She was late coming from Oxford Street where they'd taken him for a birthday treat, because he'd had one of his turns, so bad it was frightening. The seizures seemed to be getting worse, but the doctors didn't seem bothered, or even interested. A friendly cabbie had taken Darren and her mum home – no charge, and no name to thank him later. She was so grateful.

"Nothing much, just chill out," she says. "Anyway, what do you do on your days off? What about weekends?"

"I often see someone in a kind of hospital," he replies.

Carly screws up her face. "Oh, I hate hospitals. Who do you have to see, then?"

"Oh, just someone. My sister's little boy, actually. He's been ill for many years, and his father's dead."

"My brother Darren's often in a sort of hospital. He's not ill. Not ill like sick, but he's a bit slow. They let him out a lot. I really hate big hospitals – all those sick people."

"I'm sure they don't want to be sick and in hospital. Particularly if they think they're going to upset you."

Carly looks as if she was about to cry. What a drama she's making of all this, he thinks, we're only stuck in a lift! But he doesn't want more tears and so he asks her what she was planning to do for her summer holidays.

"Don't know, yet," says Carly. "We'll leave it to the last moment, as usual. Where are you going?"

"To the usual villa in Tuscany, it's nice and quiet there. We like that and it's helpful for my nephew, Oliver."

"We took Darren away to Spain, with us, once. He's at home most of the time and it was getting Mum down."

"That was good of you." In spite of himself there's something about her he likes, and he meant it kindly, but it didn't come out like that. *Not that she'd notice*, he thought.

Carly hates being patronised. "Yeah, but he really spoilt it. We met these cool people and Darren likes a drink, he's a riot when he's had a few. But he got a bit out of control, and ran away, and there was trouble with the police. We had to come home early. It's not fair, is it?"

"I'm sure you're right," he says, looking around, for he's had enough of this talk. "I'd use my mobile now, but I've forgotten it," he says breaking the unpleasant silence that's growing up around them.

"Use mine," she says, rummaging around in her bag.

He takes it, standing up, and speaks to his office. His PA gets back quickly, confirming that the lift engineers will be there within the hour. Maurice, greatly relieved, bends down to tell Carly, who is still sitting on the floor. As he does so notices that she's trembling.

"Are you rude and mean to everyone or is it just me?" she cries looking up at him, tears streaming down her cheeks. "Because if it's me, I don't see what I've done to deserve it! Don't you understand, I'm so frightened, and if anything happens to me how will they cope at home? I'm all they've got!"

Maurice gasps, nobody has said anything like that to him for years. He feels most peculiar, for it's as if someone has switched on a light, and in its glare, Carly has been stripped bare of all the trappings of inferiority with which he's invested her. For the first time, it seems, he actually *sees* a real flesh and blood human being in front of him. Someone desperately vulnerable, but still caring and selfless. Intense, unsought feelings surge about inside his mind, all jumbled up with a host of unfamiliar visceral emotions. He grasps the brass rail to steady himself.

"I'm sorry," he manages to choke out, at last. "I'm so, so

sorry. It's not you, it's not, it's really not. It's just been one of those days." How utterly pathetic that sounded! A little understanding and kindness was all she needed, anyone but a cretin could have seen that. And what had she got from him? Snide sneers from a posturing snob, taking out his own unhappiness on a vulnerable 'inferior'. Had he really thought of anyone but himself in the lift? Or anybody else recently for that matter? Or ever? He slumps back against the wall, aware that he's out of his comfort zone.

"Come on," he says, gently, "let me put my jacket round your shoulders. We're going to be here for a while. Let's start again, please borrow my handkerchief."

"I've already got it," says Carly, in a muffled, pathetic voice.

He feels like giving her a friendly little cuddle, which, of course, she senses. But that wouldn't do it for someone as attractive as her, which she also knows. She cheers up a little.

"My name's Maurice," he says, "and you're Carly. It's written on your bracelet, and I can read, too. But unlike you, I need these specs."

They both laugh and the tension between them relaxes a little. To his surprise he wants to know more about her, and asks her about her life. No one has wanted to do that in a long while and she tells him, simply and without self-pity. He learns of a life with little money, a desperate single mother and a handicapped brother, although some instinct warns her not to talk about her stepfather's abuse. Maurice hears about her comprehensive school, and her great love of maths. How one of her teachers, recognising her talent, got her accepted into the sixth form of her local grammar school, and how the other girls laughed at her accent, her clothes and her ignorance of things she'd never been taught.

Maurice is familiar with the facts of poverty – he's read the colour supplements. But he doesn't really *know* it. How could he? All his working life he's been involved with finance, and knows that money needs prudent handling. But you have to have enough in the first place to use it wisely or waste it. He's never had any real money problems in his life, nor has he grown up or worked with anyone who did. And with it came opportunity, contacts and culture but without it...

He finds it hard to put that into words, but he tells her anyway. She brightens up, and he's pleased. But what intrigues him most about her is her feeling for maths. He has a good degree in pure maths, and all his life he's worked with numbers and figures, the friends who've never let him down. He wonders how competent she was, probably just good at party piece stuff. He hopes not.

"What do you like most about maths?" he asks.

"Numbers speak to me," she says.

"Can I give you one and hear what it says?" he asks, instantly regretting it.

"Yes, all right. It'll help to pass the time," she replies, her eyes bright with interest. "Give me any number, and I'll try to do something interesting with it."

How pretty she is, he thinks and his stomach gives a little lurch.

He pauses for a moment, and then remembers the four-figure number of the cab he'd taken that morning. Nothing remarkable about it, but he gives it to her, anyway. After a pause she looks down at the floor. "It's difficult – I don't know for certain."

"It's virtually impossible, springing it on you, like that," he hastens to say, feeling wretched, and wishing he'd never started it.

"Oh no, it's quite an interesting number." She tells him why and gives him an answer. "But there may be something more, as well. Check my figures while I try out another line of approach."

He needs to use his calculator and rechecks her solution. Bloody hell, he thinks. He's confident about his own mathematical ability, but she's in a different league, and he knows that for sure, not just because he wants it to be so.

"You have great natural ability," he says.

"Yes, I have," Carly replies disarmingly immodest, "but you need proper training too, and I haven't had it."

"But Carly, surely you did well in exams," Maurice says. "You could have gone to university." She stiffens, bites her lip and turns to him, close to tears again. *For Christ's sake*, he says to himself, *think, man, before you speak*.

"Yes, Maurice, you'd think so, wouldn't you," she said. "Exams weren't a problem for me, and they put me in for this scholarship. I had to go for this interview and my mum went with me. We were so scared because no one told us what to expect. The other five candidates seemed to know one another, and they were all laughing behind our backs, but we didn't know why. And Mum had bought a special dress for me to wear, which I knew she couldn't afford, and she lost a day's pay to be there."

"So where did you go with your mum?" asks Maurice. "Your local college?"

"Oxford University. It was horrible and I hated it. When we arrived, this man called a porter asked if Mum had come for the job in the kitchens. She was so ashamed. 'Oh, Carly, I'm letting you down, after all you've done,' she said. 'Mum,' I said, 'I don't give a stuff about them. And what I've done is nothing to what you've done for Darren and me.' And we hugged each other.

"Anyhow this man, who seemed friendly, welcomed all six of us, and then we did some tests, which weren't that hard, and I finished before the others. We waited for the results and three of the others were asked to go into another room, and we didn't see them again. Then I was interviewed by the first man and two other dons, as they call them, all dressed up in gowns, sitting behind a table in a room with wood panelling.

"One was fat and leery, and he handed me an old book in Latin called *Principia Mathematica*. He said, 'You know things in this book, but what do you know about the man who wrote it? Don't be afraid, I won't expect a translation – the squiggly bits will be all Greek to you.' The others laughed, including the one who acted nicely in the first place. Lucky I knew something about Newton, wasn't it?"

Maurice recognises the breed: their smugness, cruelty and the poverty of their lives. Brilliant at first, then the long intellectual decline and now sour, superannuated husks, getting half-cut every night at the high table of some dull, unfashionable college. Spewing out the acid bile of their unfulfilled lives over vulnerable and attractive young people. When he'd met them and taken their measure, he'd retreated into his head, and kept it well down. And he'd had much more armour through his schooling and well-heeled background than she'd ever had.

"Go on, Carly," he says.

"Then there was the thin one with a runny nose and horrible veiny hands, who asked me to talk about a book I'd read recently. I could only think of *Doctor Faustus*, which we'd done in German, but I couldn't remember how to pronounce Goethe. It came out all wrong and that really creased them up. Then they asked me other things about my life, and suddenly it was all over."

"The one I'd seen first then came round the table, put his hand on my shoulder, and said to the others, 'Well, whatever else, I would certainly "sport my oak" for her.' And that set them off again, and the fat one had foam around his mouth, and the thin one was coughing up phlegm. They were just horrible. When I got outside I found Mum, who'd been looked after by the porter in his lodge, and he told her that I'd had the worst of the bunch. He said that the master and the other fellows were younger and much nicer."

"Yes, there are good ones. Those who really want to bring out the best in you," Maurice says, thinking fondly of his tutor, who befriended him so well and died so young. "So what happened when you heard from the college?"

"When I got home I told Mum that I was finished with maths, school and Oxford. So I didn't open the letters I got from the college, even though they sent them recorded delivery. And the school tried to get in touch with me, but I'd left by then, and I told them I was going away."

"Did you destroy them?" Maurice asks, gently.

"I kept them, although I knew they didn't want me. I didn't even open them."

"Why not?"

" I didn't want to give them the satisfaction of knowing that I wasn't good enough for them."

"Where are they now?"

Carly holds up her hand. "Shh… listen," she says. "What's that noise?"

Maurice looks at her and they both listen intently. They hear a squealing noise, as if a hawser is being stretched tighter and tighter, followed by a deep-throated twang. The noise stops, the lift seems to free itself, all is quiet but then it lurches violently. Maurice and Carly feel themselves slipping and sliding sideways and hold one another tightly. Then the cage rights itself, and all is still and silent.

Maurice disentangles himself from her and gropes for his glasses, which have fallen to the floor. Carly finds them and gives them back to him. The lift creaks again, so softly, and begins to swing from side to side, gently at first, and then more violently. There's the sound of shearing metal. They hold their breaths and for an instant, nothing happens. And then, like a wet dog emerging from the water, the cage begins to shake and slide free of whatever is holding it, until, with a tearing groan, it breaks away, and plummets, faster and faster.

"Christ," cries Maurice, pulling Carly towards him and holding her tight as they plunge downwards, hitting the bottom of the shaft with an explosion of sound, and a terrible jarring crunch. Lethal shards of sharp wood and jagged metal erupt around them, and then the sky falls in. Maurice feels a searing pain in his left leg, senses the roof crashing down, and lies trapped beneath a mass of metal and wood.

"Carly!" he cries. "Get her out! Get Carly out first!"

He hears someone say: "She's safe. Hold on, honey, you're doing just fine." Was that Blossom?

Then a deeper voice saying, "Don't you worry, mate, you'll

be all right. You hold my hand and squeeze it while we take this off you, we'll soon have you out." He just makes out the shape of one of the painters and wants to thank him. Then there's the prick of a needle, and he feels so tired.

★ ★ ★

He's surprised to learn how long he was unconscious, after they got him out, and it's some time after they amputated his left foot that he knew about it. Carly comes to see him regularly and sees his suffering, for it takes him a lot longer to recover than he thought it would.

"You worried that girl of yours to death, you know," says a nurse, after one of Carly's visits to him in hospital. "Always coming in to see if you were conscious. Told me she owed you her life. 'Well, anyone would do that for his daughter, wouldn't they?' I said. She got quite shirty. 'He's not my father,' she said. Isn't she a lovely girl, though?"

He gets used to the other nurses teasing him about his pretty daughter. He even jokes about it with her, but she doesn't seem to think it's funny. He thinks that's strange, for they share a sense of humour and much else besides. He notices that she uses a lot less make-up than when they first met, and dresses differently, too. But whatever she wore she would light up the whole room for him, when she appears. One day she brings Darren, who asks him what's it's like to have only one foot. "Good for hopping," he says, and Carly's eyes fill with tears. He likes Darren a lot.

When he was up and surprisingly agile with his stick, they go on meeting. Once or twice a week they eat in a pub that becomes their favourite. She's given up her job at PI and is temping somewhere or other, but there are no details of what she does or where she does it, and he doesn't enquire.

"Why don't you open one of the letters from the Oxford College?" he asks one evening. "Can't do any harm now, can it? I'll hold your hand while you do it."

She shoots him a quick glance. "I'll bring one next week, and I don't need a hand," she says. She leaves early that night and Maurice, who looks forwards so much to seeing her each week, is worried sick. He wonders if their friendship is over and that makes him want to see more of her than ever. But he's too shy to ask, for it might spoil everything. He wishes he knew women better. And when she opens the letter they found that she was offered an open scholarship in mathematics.

"Oh, my God," Carly gasps. "At last, at last, now I know. But I couldn't have taken it up. Who would have looked after Darren and Mum?"

"But you could take it up now," says Maurice. "Now listen, carefully. I didn't know until I saw the letter but it's my old college, and I know the master and the fellows well, because the company has sponsored some bursaries there, over the years. At least let me speak to them. Say I can. Please."

"Dear Maurice, you've forgotten my family."

"Oxford has short terms, and it's not that far away. Anyway, there are weekends, and I'm here. I'll look after them, I promise. You must go for it, Carly. You owe it to yourself, you just must."

"But we won't see so much of each other, either. Oh, Maurice it's all too difficult."

"No, it's not. Let's have some champagne, and drink to the future!"

And so Carly takes up her place, and Maurice, as good as his word, makes sure Darren and her mother are safe and well. He doesn't tell Carly that he pays for the best medical advice to help Darren, or that he persuades her mother to accept his help in taking breaks away. And he doesn't tell her that, after she's been home for a weekend, and they say goodbye, it's like a terrible knife twisting in his stomach. Even though when they part, he only gives her a peck on the cheek.

★ ★ ★

Time goes on, and Maurice becomes haggard with worry and despair. He's convinced Carly will meet someone of her own age and intellect, she'll be swept off her feet and he'll never see her again. He sees her in bed with a young, intellectual sophisticate, and writhes with pain at the thought, never thinking that a mature woman might have little interest in some gauche twenty-year-old. But he's hurtling on an emotional roller-coaster journey, taking months to get to the stage that ordinary starters take twenty years to reach. How she would laugh if she knew what he was going through! He feels dejected, old, crippled and useless, his work suffers, and he loses weight.

Carly's concerned about him. He'd looked a lot younger since growing his hair longer, and wearing contact lenses, but now he looks so tired and careworn. She tackles him one evening at dinner. It's her birthday and Maurice has given her a blank cheque to buy an outfit, and arranged for them to dine at a smart restaurant. She looks ravishing in her new black dress.

"Maurice, you don't look at all well, these days," she says, as dessert arrives. "It's lovely coming out like this, and I appreciate it so much. But you don't owe me anything, you know. And if you're miserable at us meeting so regularly, if it's upsetting you in some way, you'd tell me, wouldn't you?"

He's speechless. What he's been dreading, has come at last! She's found someone and wants him out of her life. What did he expect? What has he to offer someone like her? But at least he can make it easier for her, and he'll even try and retain a shred of dignity in doing it.

"Yes, Carly, it's probably better we don't go on meeting like this," he says, not meeting her eye.

She looks down into her wineglass. "It's because you've found someone and she's jealous of us, isn't it?" She sounds bitter and furious, and he's taken aback, for he's not seen her like this before. "If it is, they don't have to bother – there's nothing going on, is there, Maurice? Or likely to either. So you can tell her that from me!" She bursts into tears, pushes back her chair, and stands up to go. People look round at the noise.

Maurice is totally surprised, shocked and then delighted, as the light dawns. He leaps to his one foot, with arms outstretched, and falls heavily, pulling the tablecloth with him as he goes down. Carly falls on her knees to help him, and she's in his arms, and he's holding her as if he never wants to let her go. And that seems to be all right with her. He just can't believe how lucky or happy a human being can be. He's so enraptured, he almost forgets to pay the bill.

★ ★ ★

Carly does well at Oxford and is offered a research fellowship with dining rights at her college. And one of the first things she does when she gets the offer is to invite her mum to meet her tutor, and then take her down to the kitchens, where she says: "All this could have been yours, Mum," and they hug and laugh.

Darren is much better now. He gets on well with Maurice's nephew, Oliver, calls his sister's husband 'hop-along', and is expert at dodging whatever gets thrown at him for saying it. When he's had a few drinks in company, Maurice smiles at Carly, which he does a lot, and says, "We fell for each other, first in a lift-shaft, and then in a restaurant." He thinks it's witty, but she just smiles back, and tells him to shut up. She doesn't need reminding that Maurice always tells the truth and knows, too, that a girl may have to go to dramatic lengths to get it out of men like him. And when it works, she's found out what she'd hoped: that it can pay off, and pay off handsomely, for everyone concerned.

Beyond the Field

I suppose most people who've visited the centre would remark on its spiritual quality, but for me it's the silence and the setting that draw me back. Silence is golden, they say, and it's important for me in a way I can't fully explain. I recall reading that a famous physicist 'saw' equations in colour. Well, silence is like that for me, somehow I sense it in the round, and the centre is the place where I feel it most strongly. As for my feeling about its setting, I'll leave that to my description of the countryside in which it stands, and which I know so well.

The place wouldn't exist at all if a scruffy native child, possessing an unusual 'aura', hadn't been spotted on an Indian beach in 1909, by a well-connected Western psychic, and then groomed to be a world teacher. His benefactors lived to see him reject that role, but witnessed the start of a life devoted to addressing the big issues of life and death, meaning and reality.

When he was over ninety he was still teaching what must have seemed an endless repetition of the truths in which he believed, and pleading for harmony between all mankind. It wasn't always easy to follow his arguments, and I confess I often lost patience with him, at times finding his message verbose and confusing. I've always thought this stemmed from a lively and powerful, but untrained mind, not helped by a 'flower power' following in the California of the sixties, which I suspect he neither sought nor wanted. But he was instrumental in creating both the centre and a nearby school, whose philosophy of learning seems liberating and sincere, and I admire and respect him for these.

The centre itself, designed by an architect of vision and constructed in the 1980s, has spacious common rooms with high ceilings supported by octagonal pillars of English oak. You can stay here in simply furnished single bedrooms, and study in the library if you like, where you'll find many of the founder's books, videos and tapes. The school, run independently of the centre, has its nucleus in an eighteenth-century mansion.

The place hasn't changed in any important way over the years I've known it. It's weathered poorly and is less attractive as a structure, but now blends in more comfortably with the Hampshire countryside. That doesn't vary much either, or at least any more than is natural with the seasons. The resident staff are much as they always were: gentle, polite and friendly, in the rather distant way that often characterises spiritually inclined people. Visitors still come from many nations, and are often more practical and hard-headed than so-called 'worldly' folk might expect.

There's a great sense of acceptance here, a lack of judgement. If you want to talk, someone will listen, if you want to be alone, that's how it will be. I like that. I don't come here to make friends, but if others want to talk at mealtimes I'll usually give them my attention. I recall an Irishman bellowing away at breakfast, whilst others listened quietly, and escaping as soon as I could. Yet nothing he said was offensive, he was merely discordant and out of place. Others can be too intense and earnest for my taste, and it's best for me to leave them well alone. That's why I never attend study groups or workshops.

I usually come in the winter and walking in the countryside fills my daylight hours, for I find the atmosphere in the centre during the day rather leaden. So very different from the evening calm, when I can relax, tired from tramping through mud and brambles. In the short days I'll walk alone for hours, keeping up a steady pace and although I can cope with cold and wet conditions, sometimes it can be hard going. Often by three o'clock, when the light begins to fade, I feel I've spent a long day hiking when all I've done is five miles.

One of my favourite walks is over the fields to a tiny village nestling beside a large country house with an important twentieth-century garden. I'll start by walking past the school and into the grove, a contrived eighteenth-century wood, where you can find sequoias and other exotic redwoods embedded in a mass of rhododendrons and surrounded by an iron fence, which is covered by chicken wire to keep out the birds and animals. Hidden amongst the trees I'll stand quietly in one or two special glades, and think of the other times I've been here. I've seldom met anyone in the wood, although everyone staying at the centre will always say they've been there.

After the grove, which I leave through a gate on a fierce counterweight, I'll walk across an open field with rabbits bouncing away, little flashes of white disappearing into the hedgerows. And in the season there are pheasants here by the score, scudding away at your approach, indignant and upright, like fussy duchesses. Once, crossing the field, I saw one trapped in the space between the fence and the wire and before it broke free, marvelled at its surprising beauty.

This field can be muddy and miserable but it's a prelude to an even worse one. Large and exposed, this always has a planted crop, whether ripe and ready, or newly sown and scanty, and a path, measuring just over 500 of my paces, runs dead across its centre. The way always seems wet and slippery, with leaden, clinging soil weighing down my boots, making them feel clammy and sodden. Notices on either side of the path tell you to keep out of the field, and everything, including the awkward, rusty entrance gate seems to say you're here on sufferance. I crossed the field once in late summer after heavy rain, poorly equipped for wet conditions, forcing my way through the remains of a crop of rape, whose blackened stalks dripped with moisture, and ended up, soaked to the skin, cold and miserable. And ever since

I've harboured a resentment against these disagreeable acres and their inhospitable, unknown owner.

Then, beyond the field, comes the reward: a number of footpaths intersect, and you're overlooking a valley in gently undulating, wooded countryside, the characteristic look of this part of rural Hampshire. Trees and hedgerows are here in abundance, but settlements are sparse. Large, efficient estates dwarf the few farms, and even these have large holdings and many acres. When plants are in leaf the overall effect is misleading, for this tree-rich landscape, crossed with lanes and dotted with estate cottages, looks heavily populated, but it's not. Some say that's because of the Black Death, and perhaps the disease was worse here, or rapacious landholders moved in before people could reoccupy their villages. I'm sure mediaeval sources will show scholars what really happened, but as for me, I'll go on tramping through the lanes and the fields, simply enjoying the leafy English countryside.

My route now takes me down a descending footpath and after a few hundred metres I strike off to the right, following the line of a long hedgerow of hawthorn. This leads to a little path on one side of an earthen bank, flanked on both sides by small trees, shrubs and plants. You can easily miss it, as I did when I first came this way, but in summer or winter it's there, hidden away among the moss-covered elderberry bushes, and sturdy sycamore saplings.

Here I can stroll along rather than stride out, which I feel compelled to do in the wider countryside. The light is dim after the glare of the open fields, and objects are near at hand, unlike the far-off features of the larger field-scape. All around me, as if on a beach, is the residue of countryside life: feathers and bones, snail shells, scrapings and natural litter. But there are few signs of animals actually living here. The bank on the right, sheltering the walk, would be ideal for foxes, badgers or rabbits. But where are the burrows? Where is the disturbed earth? And where are the birds' nests? Is our countryside so sanitised and crop-saturated that birds and animals have been squeezed out?

Eventually the trees thin out and then disappear, and I find myself walking in open country again. But this is a perilous place, for I've entered the realm of the dog walker. There are access paths leading up from a main road below the flank of the hill, and here pets have free rein over the fields, and hunting rights over strangers. There can hardly be a serious walker who has not felt threatened by some ill-trained dog and its maladroit owner. Some are not intimidated, but I'll take evasive action every time.

At last the road drops down past a farm into the little village, near the large country house with its well-kept gardens, and wonderful views over the countryside. And here, too, is the little church with its small but striking contemporary stained glass windows, depicting the Pillar of Cloud and the Pillar of Fire.

I remember two acts of kindness from the people here. Once, having finished my usual walk and meaning to visit the church, I found a bent old lady sweeping the flagstones in the porch. I was diffident about entering and spoiling her work, for my boots were thick with mud, but she welcomed me in, and even offered to fetch information about the windows. I entered, looked around and, when I made to go, she'd finished sweeping. As I said goodbye she confided how shaky she'd felt all morning, and how much she wanted to go home and have a nice cup of coffee. We agreed that would work wonders, but I'd like to have done more for her than just be friendly. I was greatly touched by this kind, frail person, who had welcomed me in the same spirit that had made her turn out to tidy up the church, when it was probably the last thing she felt like doing.

The gardens were closed when I reached the house, and I was disappointed, for the topiary was freshly shaped, the trees looked trim and the walkways so inviting. I asked a gardener if I might look at the kitchen gardens, and he invited me, with genuine warmth, to look at everything in the main grounds as well. Alone in such a garden with its sweeping views was not something easily forgotten, and neither was his kindness. How these trivial events stick in the mind, for good or for ill! I remember not entering a pub for thirty years because the landlord was once off-hand when we went there. And who has not been influenced by a chance remark for years, even when lightly uttered?

After the village there's the long walk back to the centre and sometimes a last look at the grove. I went there once with a tall, loose-limbed Dutch woman, who practised some kind of yoga in the nearby grounds, contorting her rangy body into attitudes that made her resemble a giant crane. At dinner she confided to me that she'd recently lost a relative and another guest, who I suspect was a psychiatrist, advised her to think of him in a favourite place. I felt how powerful such simple advice can be when loss is recent, pain is raw, and there's an aching void in your life. The man plainly wanted to be off duty, but had offered help to someone who needed it.

I liked her a lot, for she used to nip off and smoke in the bushes. As I had smuggled in a tiny portable TV to shorten what could be very long days, I felt a warm affinity for this fallible fellow human. But now I don't need these devices so much.

However often you visit the centre it's always the people you meet there who surprise you. I met an affable Indian once, who told me he lived under a tree, 3,000 metres up in the Himalayas, and used forest plants to augment his diet, but was sometimes concerned about dangerous wild dogs. He seemed utterly sincere and totally unbelievable. He'd just completed a rail journey from Beijing to Mongolia, and trips like that didn't come cheap. When I asked him how these travels came about, he said they "just did". The next day he was leaving to fly to Delhi and I offered to take him to Winchester. Although he said he only needed dropping by the station, when we got there he knew exactly where he wanted to be, and that was with a friend, a well-known author of Hampshire travel books. I wished him a pleasant flight, and when we parted found that he was travelling business class.

One day I had finished a long walk and was making my way through the kitchen garden of the school when I felt very ill. I collapsed when I reached my room, and lay on the floor, wondering if the pain could get any worse and how long it would last. I had good reason to worry for, unknown to me, I had severe heart disease. Indeed my condition had become so serious that I was operated on within a few days of a diagnosis. So I avoided going back to the centre, for I associated being there with negative thoughts of pain, panic and fear.

When I decided to lay the ghost and return, I found that the place hadn't changed much, the same people were there, and the countryside was familiar. But I was sadder and more withdrawn than before; although, for some reason, more at peace with my surroundings. And the centre still had something else important to offer, for in its heart is a quiet room. You are invited to go there and carry into it the peace you have acquired during at least a few days' stay. It's an earned right, which is the best sort, and feels good to leave something helpful to others, as others have helped you. I've seen it abused by a day visitor who wanted to steal its peace for his own selfish meditation, but that's just human nature.

Now here's an odd thing. Although I felt no closer to the founder and his teachings, at the same time I was feeling increasingly at home with the centre, sympathetic to its aims and appreciative of the way it was run. And then I learned something about him I'd not heard before.

Only ten days before his death, this man, then well over ninety, who'd spent all his life addressing reality in one form or another, said that nobody had ever understood him or his teachings. I'm sure he said this without rancour or regret. He was in good company: even Jung said that he'd had to hint at things which others knew nothing of, and for the most part did not want to know. And Wittgenstein said something similar about his philosophy. He felt he was writing for people who would think in a different way, and breathe a different air from those of the present day. His work was for those to come, not for those who were living.

The insight of the centre's founder made me want to sit alone in the grove with him, a special place for both of us, and together feel the peace of the place. I'd want to let him feel what I'm sure he already knew: that in spite of being misunderstood, his achievement was real. It's just that for me its purest expression was not in speech or writing, but in the healing silence and quiet reflection that his vision had made possible. And how it helped me understand what Wittgenstein meant when he said, "Whereof one cannot speak, thereof one must be silent."

The Ends of the Earth

The ends of the earth. Far, far away, or much nearer than
you think? Mysterious, unfathomed places? Every night in
your sleep, you visit them. Real places, then, that you feel
are empty and desolate? But wouldn't anywhere that generates
similar feelings qualify, whether they're far away or near at hand?
I think so, for to me, the ends are more than just physical, far-
off locations. They're places of absent or vanished intimacy: the
room in a dismal city bedsit where someone has choked out the
last breath of a lonely life; the strangely unoccupied bed in the
now-empty sickroom; the lonely walk along a familiar, formally
shared way. Are these places not every bit as desolate as the tent
where Scott died in his 'dreadful place' in the Arctic?

Take Shimla, high up in the mountains of Northern India,
once the summer residence of the British Raj, and come back
with me to 1947. Watch the very last column of British soldiers
march through the choking dust, before boarding the train down
to the scalding plains, leaving behind empty buildings, perched
upon high and mighty terraces. Imagine now, the Indians,
wandering with impunity into the echoing rooms, reclaiming
their own. No thought of forlornness for them in those empty
rooms, for places that have been occupied and not truly lived in,
become merely vacant when people have gone. When I last saw
Shimla it had been lived in and was truly Indian – chaotic, dirty,
patched up and overrun by monkeys. Former officials of the Raj,

seeing it as I did, would undoubtedly regard it as forlorn, for all traces of a way of life, once giving meaning to their own, had gone.

Now let's take a trip on the Docklands Light Railway to the far fringes of East London, where it merges with the countryside proper. Not the worn greenery of well-meant municipal parks, squeezed in between the wars and cramped amongst building developments, but where the sky spreads out, clouds clothe far horizons, and the east wind blows fresh and keen, replacing the gritty gusts of the City.

Go almost to the end of the line, nearly to Beckton, where the greatest sewage outfall in Europe disgorges into the Thames, and get out at Gallions Reach. Then, you'll find yourself stranded and alone in a large, flat and impersonal space. But it's not the estuary and mud you're wading in, but standing puzzled on a vast mass of concrete, radiating from a huge roundabout. And there's good cause to feel lost, for nothing tells you where you are, or points to where you might want to go. Perhaps because there's nowhere the authorities might imagine anyone would want to walk to from here.

Ignore them, the planners and developers, and use your senses to direct you. You'll smell that water's near, and bet it's going to where the concrete towers are highest, so that tiny balconies, clinging to blocks of purpose-built flats, can boast a river view. And you're right. Cross two roads like great empty runways, and there's the water. Hardly Thames water but still river water, now tamed, free from salty surges and tidal reach. It's stretched out before you, ranks of wind-flecked waves, marshalled in neat lines, meekly contained within walls half a mile long. You've found the mighty Royal Albert Dock, but there's no sign of the river that bred and feeds it. That's nearby, though: a great body of estuarine water, swelling and receding, silently shifting a million tons of cold mud and soggy sand.

Then, in the midst of the cheap, hasty new-build you catch sight of a lone building. It's stood there for 130 years, the last fifty empty and unwanted, dwarfed now by the concrete towers which surround it. A neo-Elizabethan hotel with elaborate mouldings, half timbers and a red roof. Victorian passengers from the Empire, if they had the means and the inclination, would rest here before resuming their journeys either east for duty, or London for leave. Now it's empty and forlorn, and there's little to hint at its past – those last embraces and dubious homecomings, the loss and the relief, and all the paraphernalia of travel.

Here the vanished human presence is so profound. A lingering Victorian flavour of wretchedness and hapless, conditioned sacrifice. Boys wrenched from their families in India at eight, to live alone with strangers, often bullied and always denied the expression of emotion. Unhappy until they were old enough to escape the bonds, and then repeating the process, in the name of duty to masters ruling a country they were supposed to love and for which many of them died.

And here there were also those, less well born, whose youth and health were plucked from them, loading and unloading cargoes, by hand and muscle, to line the pockets of those whose ships docked here. Men working barefoot, who before the dock strike of 1889 spent the 5d they earned for an hour's work on food to keep them going for the rest of the day. But now there's only a stretch of desolate water that once held hundreds of ships, an abandoned hotel and new roads that run nowhere special. There's a deep sadness in the air here, not just a residue of the sorrows of the well born, or the hopelessness of the early dock workers. Perhaps it's a memory of the *Princess Alice* disaster of 1878, when an overloaded pleasure boat was rammed by a collier, and over 600 day trippers drowned in the infected water below the great sewer outfall. Think of those pretty dresses, billowing out for an instant, and then dragging the girls in their heavy, wet shrouds, down into the dark, contaminated depths.

If you're lucky someone will have left a rusty gate open, and you can walk the northern length of the great watery basin, all alone. Far enough to be away from any traffic on the roads, and quiet enough to feel the wind in your ears blowing across the long, flat fetch of water. You'll walk along a cracked and ancient concrete way, peppered with scraggy ragwort, plastic bottles and wind-blown litter. Far away to the east rise the great walls of Canary Wharf, whose unlikely shapes, slopes and distorted reflections muddle the mind and dazzle the eye. From here it looks ethereal, like a poetic vision of Troy, and strangely ephemeral too, for although these gigantic structures are as heavy as the Thames is wet, this is less an eternal city than an eternal building site.

These distant, beautiful buildings housing vibrant life and energy, contrast sharply with the derelict dock past which you are walking. And now, away to your left on the opposite bank, rather surprisingly, is an airport. This is another piece of the forlorn jigsaw, for here all is arrival and departure, with its keen sense of joy and reunion, but also separation and sadness, too.

Perhaps those drawn to forlorn places savour their lingering, bitter-sweet sadness and here, on the edge of a great city, you have it all in spades. The remoteness of the river and its surroundings, the 'end of the line' feeling in getting there, the cold concrete that awaits you, and the old hotel saying: "I am without purpose, keep me if you must, but let me live again." Then the empty dock, where few birds swim or dive, the distant City buildings, massive and vulnerable and the planes taking off and landing. All this, and the rusty wire fence amongst the cast-off cartons, rubbish, and scruffy yellow weeds, to bring you back to earth!

Do emotions linger after people disappear? Not always. I've studied ruined pyramids and empty temples from Stonehenge to Mexico, Peru to Thailand, often with admiration but always without emotion. But just the photograph in Hiroshima of a pair of broken spectacles rescued from a ruined house touched me deeply. And in the London Blitz what could be more forlorn than a bombed building, revealing small intimate details of the lives of its residents, their lives stripped bare, exposed to the passionless gaze of prurient passers-by? Go to a great mansion and it's the rooms below stairs, like the little kitchen with its sixties' radio and well-used but unoccupied chair by the electric fire that touches the heart, not the empty staterooms, high above. Enter a church, isolated in a meadow for generations, because of enclosures, and listen in your mind to the lost, homely voices raised in prayer. Walk through little abandoned villages in Croatia, where an earthquake forced people to go down to the coast, heartbroken to have to leave their family homes. Visit a shack abandoned in the Antarctic with all the daily objects left, just as they were last used, and now abandoned. Look at a little boarded-up shop, now empty and valueless, and think about the dreams and hopes that were wrapped up in its early days, and the anguish that haunted its decay into disuse. And feel the tension and the terror trapped for ever in war trenches, and silent, disused airfields.

All of these once had a human presence, strong as birdsong, now absent as a kindly impulse in a shopping sale. Hadrian's Wall's still got it, the Tower of London has lost it and the Great Wall of China never had it. And out on the farthest extremes of East London, you can still hear the choirs and long-lost litanies of pain and loss in the biting wind that skims over the cold, uncaring mud and waters. Drowning out the singers and the song, the forgotten words and the melody, unheard by most, but keenly felt by those who care enough to listen.

HAWAII

'd been unsettled since we arrived at the hotel in Kailua Bay, on the west coast of Big Island, which is what the locals call the island of Hawaii. At first I thought it was simply a reaction to having spent the last few days in Oahu, surrounded by fast-food outlets, depressing malls and a hefty dose of patriotic fervour at Pearl Harbour. But, in fact, none of those had been quite as bad as we'd feared.

So what, I wondered, could be causing this feeling of unease? The chaotic flight from Oahu? Hardly, we'd had worse. And that went for our scruffy, spacious hotel room, as well, with its worn furniture, basic plumbing and grubby balcony with the battered, plastic chairs, where small birds constantly fluttered around for food. But we had clear views out to the sea beyond the hotel's palms, where we could watch the wind-swept water to our heart's content. We would follow the low-slung, whale-watchers' boats thrashing out to sea, slipping and sliding in the heavy swell, water creaming away from their bows as they rose and plunged through the surging sea, and feel thankful that we weren't on board.

Nor was the weather to blame, so hot and humid, beneath a leaden sky. We'd expected that, and adjusted ourselves accordingly. Or the sound of the wind forcing itself through the rat-infested palm trees below us, their spiky fronds grating away, day and night. I'd heard that so many times before that now I found it almost comforting. And we'd long ago come to accept nasal, screech-pitched Californian voices, complaining and bickering, as usual in the next room.

All these, I told myself, were common irritations, familiar to those who, like us, had travelled widely. So what else might have caused such a deep-seated discomfort? I sat out on the balcony and thought. Was it the island itself that was affecting my mood, I wondered? Big Island, geologically young, is towering and remote, much younger than the Alps and, if you discount the fact that the sea covers most of its base, higher than the Himalayas. It's also further from other shores than anywhere else on earth, and the youngest and most active in the Hawaiian chain. It's moving westwards, just like its brothers and sisters, Kauai, Oahu, Molokai, Lanai and Maui, for deep beneath the bed of the Pacific, is a hot spot, a rupture in the earth's crust, from whose depths the lava spews that has given birth to them all. On Big Island it hasn't stopped yet, and the volcano Kilauea, on its western coast, is the most active in the world.

Perhaps this was the key to my unease. The forces that shape the earth are usually sheathed in secrecy. But here, geologically, work is still in progress, and the evidence of great physical processes is all around you. Does this restlessness transmit itself to those who live here, and some, like me, who visit it? The few long-term residents we met made much of their affinity to the place, as if to reassure themselves of the security of an uneasy tenure. People I met in rural Alaska were like that, for there whole slabs of countryside can suddenly sink without warning, and natural forces are evident everywhere.

These are the unmade places of the earth, land that still needs grounding. Not much chance of that here, in the middle of the Pacific, so far from the grown-up land masses that one day in the far future, it will join. So call it fanciful if you will, but I reasoned that it was the obvious working out of natural processes all around me that I found disquieting, and influenced my feelings about the island. And whenever the west wind blew volcanic plumes to smudge the clean sky, making everything feel soiled and gritty, it would remind me that we were perched on a moving raft of rock, heading ever north-west, over the great expanse of the Pacific Ocean.

But, in spite of my unease, and on another level, there were many things here to interest us. Pig roasting was one. Every morning a deep pit was prepared in the hotel grounds, wood piled inside, set alight and a whole pig placed on the flames. Then it would be covered with banana leaves, and slowly cooked all day long. In the evening for the tourists who had paid to come, the roasted pig would be disinterred, and served with thin wine in plastic cups, accompanied by traditional dancing on a small stage. We had a ring-side seat from our balcony to see the festivities. The next morning the pit was made ready again, another pig was roasted, and another evening of eating and dancing ensued.

The island seemed strangely devoid of people in the day, and we wandered around quiet malls, and rode on empty shuttle buses. We heard that tourist numbers were down, and the three cruise ships that used to come every Wednesday, were now down to one. Across 2,500 miles of empty ocean and 3,000 miles of America, decisions affecting incomes and spending, themselves reactions to wider markets, had worked down and influenced the numbers eating roast pig on the Kona Coast of an island in the remotest chain on earth.

And here there were things of beauty, too. The waters washing the small, rocky beach beyond the pig-roast area were crystal clear. Pure and sterile, for the young island hasn't built up the soil and nutrients that muddy the shorelines in more established places. And in this impoverished, beautiful sea only a yard or two from land, exotic tropical fish swim calmly, as if in an aquarium. I once saw a snake, curled up on the ribbed sand in a foot or so of water near to some local women, wading with their skirts up, and shouted a warning to them. But they just went on smiling and chatting, and seemed quite unafraid.

One day we booked to go on a trip around the island. The bus would drive round the hotels on the bay in the early morning, gathering up tourists, curious, like us, to see the big attractions. We'd be picked up at 6.30 in the morning, and knew it would be humid even then. And so, after a restless night with the air-conditioning rattling, early light seeping through ill-fitting shutters and a fierce shower with noisy plumbing, we stepped out into the warm bath of the day.

It was very quiet so early in the morning, and we walked through the silent lobby, and joined two older people waiting outside the hotel entrance. Brad and Bobbie were from Wisconsin, where they'd been farmers. Retired now, they both drove kids to school in the yellow buses you see everywhere in the States. I pictured them, driving in all weathers, along the straight, empty roads of that rural state, two people the kids will always remember. In their turn they doubtless knew all the names and natures of their young charges, and their parents as well, living in remote farms and smallholdings. They were ill at ease on Big Island, for it was expensive to eat there, and all their lives they'd had to watch the pennies. They also lacked the hollow small talk that Americans use to kindle friendships that last until the sun goes down, and we found their reticence refreshing.

We asked them if they'd visited the small mall that lined the road along the shore, down from the hotel, for we wondered what they'd made of it. It was almost deserted when we walked round it, and along with the skin therapy clinic, the cosmetic product store and the seashell emporium there was a picture gallery that sold large, original paintings. We were astonished to find that many of the works, of high quality and meticulously painted in the style of Norman Rockwell, were priced at over $100,000. But who, we wondered, would buy such things in that modest mall on an obscure spot of a tiny island in the middle of the Pacific? And more mysterious still, we found jewellery made from a jet-like substance, which became popular when Queen Victoria, in deep mourning for the death of Albert, favoured black jewellery. How could such a tradition, not even known in England, start here, let alone be perpetuated?

Brad and Bobbie seemed even more perplexed by the mall than we were, but said little and looked uncomfortable, as people often are when they're not used to meeting and talking to strangers. It was getting more humid by the minute out there by the road, and we also fell silent, reserving our conversation for the long day ahead. We longed for the bus with its air-conditioning to arrive, and grew impatient for it was late. They often are, stopping as they do, at numerous hotels to pick up people who can be unreliable. The drivers are used to picking up disgruntled passengers and can be tough nuts, as we'd already found out.

On the island of Maui there is a famously beautiful but hair-raising road that runs, hugging the coast, from the central town of Kahului, to the tiny town of Hana, on the extreme eastern end of the island. When we boarded a small tour bus to travel the road, we found that the air conditioning was set at its lowest temperature and fiercest volume. The sturdy woman driver refused to have it adjusted on the grounds that people in cold coaches are less inclined to vomit on the floor, as the tour involved negotiating demanding bends high above sheer cliffs. She told us that her job was to drive, not to minister to the sick or clean up after them. Our companions, mainly inoffensive elderly Canadians, exchanged anxious glances, and we lurched forward, tensed up and apprehensive. And true enough, there was no sickness in that icy bus as it sped along its humid, mountainous route.

Our current bus arrived and, as we squeezed into our seats we smiled at our companions. Sal the driver grunted, looked in his mirror and announced that we were now complete. About sixty years old, once lanky and raw-boned but now slack-muscled and paunchy, he wore a check shirt, a belt with an elaborate silver buckle, jeans and fancy cowboy boots. There were heavy tattoos on both of his arms, and a dense handlebar moustache, stained brown, bristled above his mouth. His creased, tanned skin set off

125

his watery blue eyes; the thinning grey hair was pulled back in a ponytail, and on the dash was a Stetson hat, which he put on, and wore for the rest of the day.

Further down the road he pulled into a lay-by, clicked on the microphone and, turning to face us, outlined where we were going, what we would see and how long it would all take. Then he told us how long he and his wife had lived on Big Island, that they'd been married for twenty-five years, described his dog and told us we would soon be passing his family home. He then asked us where we came from and we learned that, as well as Brad and Bobbie, there were four middle-aged Americans from the East Coast, a Japanese couple, and three Canadians from Toronto. And all of us were staying in hotels clustered along Kailua Bay.

Sal swung back in his driver's seat, crashed the gearbox and we jerked away onto the main road. We began to climb away from the coastline, and soon we were high enough to look back over the sea to our left, where we could see the line of hotels flanking the bay. The country we were driving through looked desolate and parched after the lush hotel gardens. Scanty clumps of coarse grass protruded from gritty, black soil between dark rocks, honeycombed and streaked with brown on the seaward side, and greenish patches of brown-edged, desiccated lichen marked where standing water had dried up in the summer heat. Soon we were passing fenced-off areas of land with the barbed wire twisted and broken between bent posts, and a few abandoned-looking shacks surrounded by rusty farm machinery and ancient cars, the ground criss-crossed with deeply indented tyre tracks.

The road climbed higher still, and when it levelled out we were crossing a great palette of once-molten rock, rising inland towards a thick line of trees, beyond which rose the brooding bulk of the volcano Hualalai. The road skirted the lower part of this plateau of black rocks, which in one place were jumbled and jagged, and in another shiny, smooth and almost liquid looking. Scanty trees protruded from this thick patination on the earth's surface, looking frail and vulnerable, as if aware that the rocks might suddenly exert on them a suffocating pressure.

Sal shifted his weight and spoke into the microphone. Now that we were underway he relaxed and took charge. A guide I greatly respected told me that North Americans expected you, as a guide, to keep talking all the time you were travelling with them. Sal kept up the great tradition, patronising, amusing and informing us from the beginning, and running through everything he said was the recurrent theme of his wife.

It started as we crossed the black laval plain. He pointed over to the right, up near the line of trees and far away, where there was a clapperboard house, incongruously built in the middle of a sea of solidified lava. That's where he lived with his wife and dog, he told us, where she was always complaining, and the dog was always whining. He sounded the horn to tell them he was passing and asked us all to wave. We looked at each other, self-consciously and then we flapped limp hands but there was no response from that odd dwelling on its hard bed of volcanic rock. Then just before I stopped waving I blinked, for didn't I see the faintest hint of something red moving inside the house? I couldn't be sure, and the moment passed, without comment.

Sal was a safe driver, considerate about stops for those who needed them, informed about the history of the island and a good raconteur of anecdote and gossip. But that didn't stop him being relentless in his constant reference to his wife. When we stopped at a Kona coffee museum we learned that she hated coffee, when we walked across beaches of fine, jet-black sand he refused to walk with us, as the sand clung to his shoes and his wife complained about the mess. But he was quiet and thoughtful when we left the bus and gazed at green and hawksbill turtles, peered down the smoking Kilauea caldera, felt the fine spray of the rainbow falls, marvelled at the green plunging valleys of the Hamakur coast and admired the wonderful painted eucalyptus trees whilst buying nuts at a macadamia farm. But when we returned to the bus he resumed his theme. On and on about his life at home, his wife's constant nagging, his lack of an independent life. We left the bus at 7.30, after a great tour, but with our ears ringing.

There was a quiet little restaurant looking out over the hotel's bay where we used to eat most nights. There was usually a local there, some old boy chatting up the tourists for the price of a drink or two. On the night of our round trip, we found a veteran sitting alone in the little lobby, where we'd enjoy a nightcap, looking out over the bay at the palms outlined against the lights of the hotels. We bought him a drink and mentioned what we'd done in the day. We asked him if he knew our driver.

"Sal the Stetson – sure I know him," said the old boy. "You'll have heard all about his wife, I suppose, and his dog."

"She's rather difficult according to Sal," said my wife, "and the dog doesn't help."

"He tell you she makes him work all year round, without taking a break. He tell you that? Winter and summer, and public holidays, too?"

We nodded. "Something like that. He told us she never wants to leave the island, but he'd rather go."

"Well, she ain't going anywhere, that's for sure, and I don't suppose he will now, either."

"What keeps them here? They don't seem very happy on the island."

"His wife and the dog died in a fire, five years past, up at their place on top of the lava field. Sal was out driving, and can't forgive them for going. Not old Sal. Guess it helps when it gets bad for him that he's got people to talk to who don't know what happened. Then he can pretend she's still around, in that red dress she always wore at home in that shack. It's empty nowadays, and he never goes near it. Darndest thing."

"That's so sad," said my wife.

"Odd place, this island," said the old boy. "Don't know why, but it's not good for folk who want to hold on to things, like remembering kin they've lost. Things can slip through your fingers like sand here, if you let them. The place is always moving on, and the past can go hang. What you need here's a bit of an anchor to steady you down. And as I said, old Sal just gets a bit carried away with losing his kin, every once in a while. Can't find it in me to blame him, though."

And neither could we. But you know, I can just see a National Geographic article entitled: 'Big Island, Land on the Move', and think, what do they know? That the truth is a man in a Stetson, and a wife in a red dress? Or is it? Unsettling place, Big Island.

THE WELL

I n London, I worked from home and was finishing off the design of an extension to a house in Bloomsbury when I heard Anne coming back from her meeting with the specialist. Just a routine problem, nothing to worry about, we'd thought. The news was devastating, and we held each other closely, too numb to even weep. We'd planned to retire to the country one day, but now it seemed we'd be leaving London much sooner than expected.

The house went on the market, and we started sorting through forty years of accumulated paperwork. When my mother had died ten years before, her affairs were in such a mess that we'd let our solicitor handle most of it. And that explained why I was seeing, for the first time, documents relating to a property owned by a Great-uncle Arthur, in Henley-on-Thames. They revealed that, in the early 1930s, he'd lived with his wife in Fern Cottage, New Street, and after she died remained there, until his murder. Had we not felt so raw and obsessed with fear for the future, a death in the family like that would have intrigued us greatly. Now it hardly registered. But it did suggest that the idea of living somewhere like Henley might suit us very well, and so we went there the following weekend.

When we arrived in that high summer, the weather was oppressive and humid, and even the Thames seemed to flow sluggishly through the town. We lunched at The Angel on the

Bridge, walked past the parish church, strolled through the graveyard and ended up in New Street, which we found ran eastwards to a slipway on the river. Anne, exhausted by the heat, rested on a bench by the water, while I walked slowly along the street looking at the buildings. They intrigued me, for I could see that the Georgian facades disguised much older structures, and on the southern side stood a number of unrestored half-timbered Tudor houses. But I saw no evidence of Fern Cottage.

It was when I'd almost reached the end of the street that I spotted a narrow, enclosed passageway between two ancient houses. I stepped into this dark corridor, whose plastered walls were sweating with damp and decay, and emerged into a small courtyard, enclosed on two sides by high, ancient walls, with a circular well in its centre surrounded by a low stone wall. An ancient iron grill secured by a heavy padlock covered the opening, and although I peered down into the centre of the well, whose upper walls were lined with concentric rings of greasy, glistening bricks, I found it impossible to see anything in the black depths. But what, I wondered, had made those scratches in the wall, as if something had scraped for purchase in hauling up a heavy body? And then, catching an unpleasant foetid odour rising from below, I straightened up and for some reason looked around, but there was no one to be seen.

What I did see was a small, dirty-white cottage, set back from the well with the words 'Fern Cottage', on a sign above the door. I hastened to tell Anne what I'd found, and together we retraced my steps. But when she emerged from the passage, wrinkling her nose at the smell of damp and decay and passed the well, she put her hand to her mouth, grasped my arm and backed away. It was a violent, unexpected reaction, and one she couldn't explain. But it was clear that the well frightened and disgusted her.

The cottage was clearly unoccupied, even though peering through a grimy window I thought for a moment that I detected a movement inside. There was a battered 'For Sale' sign on the cottage wall, and we learned from the local agent that the house, a probate sale, had been on the market for some time. Perhaps because of the family connection I felt drawn to the place, and, after another visit I convinced Anne that the building was basically sound, and so cheap that we could buy it without having to wait to sell the London house. But she was still so deeply disturbed by the well's proximity to the cottage that I promised to find the owner, and have it capped off. But that proved easier said than done.

No legal records relating to the courtyard existed, and there was no mention of the well in our solicitor's search. What he did unearth were details of an underground stream running the length of New Street, before draining into the Thames. Cellars in nearby buildings routinely flooded after heavy rain, but our solicitor felt that to proceed too far with inquiries would disturb a hornet's nest. It was probable that hidden, interconnected water courses existed, and more than likely that the network extended to Hart Street, a road running parallel to New Street. I reassured Anne as best I could, and eventually she agreed to go ahead with the purchase.

By late autumn we had moved in. I was pleased that the cottage was once again back in the family, but my immediate priority was to make Anne comfortable, for every day she was getting weaker. The cottage was not ideal for an invalid, for the only way to the low-beamed bedrooms was via a flight of steep wooden stairs, and as she was finding climbing difficult I arranged a bed for her in the sitting room. It was the nicest part of the cottage, with linen-fold panels lining its walls, an oak beam spanning the entire length of the ceiling, and others running at right angles from it to the walls. An old bread oven fed into the large inglenook fireplace which, supported by its corbel of weathered brick, was large enough for a man to stand upright. If you looked up the chimney on a sunny day you could glimpse the open sky high above.

In spite of my efforts, shortly after we settled in, Anne suffered a stroke and was taken to hospital. When her condition stabilised she was unresponsive and withdrawn, and still much too ill to come home. For a while I lost all interest in life, but the mood passed, and, my fascination with old buildings returning, I began a detailed survey of the cottage.

Two things in particular intrigued me about the property. The rune-like marks deeply incised on the old beams in the bedrooms were puzzling, defeating all my attempts to identify them; and the linen-fold panelling in the living room, much too grand for the cottage, had clearly started life elsewhere. And it was behind a loose section of this woodwork that I found the diary, ending with heavily flagged-up entries from 21ˢᵗ December 1932 until Christmas Eve, four days later. Their script, originally precise and firm, degenerated badly as the days passed, and there was a scrap of paper inside on which the author had written his name. I stared at the signature, my heart thumping, for it was my uncle's. Carrying the diary over to the window, I sat down and read the last few entries, and this is my account of the story they tell.

It began one evening, a few days before Christmas 1932, and Uncle Arthur, having crossed the river, was walking home through Henley's Hart Street, making for the marketplace. His route took him along a handsome road parallel to New Street, flanked by old buildings, some of which were converted into shops.

All day a bitter wind had been blowing along the river and now, as darkness approached, a violent snowstorm fell upon the town. Uncle stumbled through the doorway of the nearest building for shelter, brushed the snow from his coat and looked around. He was in a shop that he didn't recognise, gloomy, airless and empty, and as quiet as the grave. At the back of the shop he saw a doorway covered by a thin curtain masking a dim, flickering light, and gently moving the drape to one side he passed through, into a shadowy room. The only light was coming from two candles near the door, and there were glass-fronted cabinets ranged around the walls from floor to ceiling, their shelves filled with strangely shaped vessels. There was a heavy, musky smell in the room.

"Can I help you?" said a voice.

He peered around and saw a young woman, with a pale, lovely face and huge slanting eyes, standing in the shadows.

"I'm so sorry," he stammered. "It was rude of me to come in, I'm only sheltering from the snowstorm, I don't need anything."

"Those who find their way here always need something," said the girl. "Do you want something undone? A connection you wish to make? Some advice, perhaps?"

Judging from his neat writing, I see my uncle as a rational, thoughtful man, and I picture him frowning at this. "I don't think I need any of those," he replied.

"Where do you live?" she asked, unexpectedly.

"Fern Cottage, in New Street," he said, off guard.

She looked quickly over her shoulder, and dropped her voice. "Now I understand why you're here. You're not meant to be there, and it's dangerous for you to stay. I don't know why but you're being given a chance, and so I'll give you something to protect you. But it will only save you long enough to get out of harm's way. If we meet again it will not be like this."

She went to a cabinet, took down from a shelf a small terracotta figure, with its hands in a praying position and gave it to him. "It's most kind of you, but I really didn't mean to buy anything," he said, making to hand it back.

She turned away. "It was yours from the moment you held it," she said. "When you sense danger hold it firmly, and it will protect you, but only for a moment. If you stay longer in that place, nothing can help you."

"I really can't just take it," he said, neither understanding nor believing her words.

She grasped his arm. "Then give me something in return. Quickly!"

He searched in his pockets, and found his business card.

"Evil compels others to help it gain what it most desires,"

she said, taking it, and for an instant he saw in her eyes a deep, fleeting sadness. Then he heard a noise, a kind of rustling as if something had entered and was moving in that darkling world, and she moved him swiftly towards the door.

Outside the storm had passed leaving the sky black and clear, and the air bitterly cold. Overhead stars must have winked and glittered and ice crystals in the snow would have sparkled in the streetlight's glare. Even in the thirties Uncle might have walked past horses, snorting and stamping outside the Catherine Wheel Hotel, their flanks and breath steaming in the icy air. He had an uneasy feeling of being observed, and quickened his pace.

At home he put the figurine on a side table, and regarded it. *An odd gift*, he thought. *And what of the strange meeting and her warning?* He dismissed it as fanciful. He began to write his diary, but a wind had sprung up, and a rattling window distracted him for a moment. When he'd finished, he piled more logs on the fire to try to cheer up the room.

His night was troubled: the wind moaned down the chimney keeping him awake, and he felt unwell. The next day he brought in extra supplies of food in case illness prevented him getting out. The passageway was filling up with snow and if more fell it would be completely blocked. Being hemmed in disturbed him, and he found himself constantly looking out of the window at the snow piling up around the well.

I see him, more ill than he realised, hunched up and alone, before that great fireplace in that room full of shadows and fear. In his journal he scribbled about how he senses the house awakening, preparing for something, and how vulnerable he feels. The words of the girl came back to him, but again he dismissed them. Perhaps he looked across from his armchair to the figurine on the side table. How on earth could it help him if he sensed danger? He's trapped there, ill and weak, where can he go?

Now it's two days before Christmas Eve, and in the night there were heavy footsteps on the roof. They paused and continued, for what seemed hours. What was it? What was it seeking? He listened lying there, faint and feverish, in that rumpled bed, his heart in his mouth. But in the morning there was no sign of anything unusual in the cottage or outside. He peered out of the window at the well under its burden of snow, and then he staggered back to bed, and slept and slept.

The next day he stayed in bed but in the late afternoon hunger drove him to get up. As dusk approached the lights in the cottage faltered and failed, and now there was only the candlelight to keep the dark at bay. His stock of wood was getting low as the night drew on, and he heard an icy wind whipping whirlpools of snow into freezing mounds in the courtyard. And now he's afraid to look out, for what he might see near the well. Snowflakes descended through the open chimney, thawing as they fell, and hissing and spitting as they hit the firewood. Frigid downdraughts sent icy gusts of choking smoke into the room, and he clasped his chest, rocking backwards and forwards, racked with painful coughing.

And now in the glancing firelight he saw a huge black cat with great green eyes on the stairs. He groped for his glasses, but when he looked again there was nothing there. Shouting nonsense, he hauled himself upstairs to search for the animal, but found the bedrooms empty and cold. Weak and trembling he turned to descend, missed his footing and fell to the floor of the sitting room, striking his head on the arm of the chair. He wrote, "How can I avoid what's to come?"

And then something makes him stagger to the iced-up window and pull the curtain aside. At first he saw nothing but then he made out a dark shape. Was there something out there by the well, something gaunt and angular, whose robes hung in great folds from a spare body? Was it leaning over the well helping some dark shape emerge? And as it lifted itself up, inclining towards him, was that face human, hidden within the shadow of its hood?

Much later, dozing before the fireplace, he awoke with a

start. The room was icy and something was pushing urgently against the front door. With the last of his strength he heaved a linen chest across the room, and all through that long night lay propped against it, in and out of feverish sleep. The door held, and in the morning there was no sign of anything amiss.

Now he'd scarcely eaten for days and the half-glimpsed face haunted his dreams and his waking hours, both now merging into one dreadful present. Even as the shadows of the night recede into the pale light of dawn, he knows only too well that what you resolve in daylight weakens when the shadows lengthen. Soon he fell asleep.

And then it was evening after a terrible, endless day. Unshaven and unkempt, he watched the very last logs burning low, and the darkness creeping from the corners of the sitting room. Outside the wind had shifted the snow from the well in the courtyard, leaving the black centre gaping and unprotected. Sitting before the fireplace he wrote feverishly in his journal, and when he had finished he pushed the book into the gap in the wall, and replaced the wooden panel.

With his diary finished I can only conjecture what came next. Perhaps there was a slight sound on the roof, and the cat was on the stairs, twitching its tail, alert and expectant. Possibly something was moving in the garden. Might he now have reached out for the figurine, but his hands fumbled and it fell to the hearth, smashing into fragments. Then a scraping noise came from the chimney, soot fell onto the carpet, and his business card fluttered down. He leant forward in his chair, picked up a poker from the hearth, took from his pocket his mother's crucifix and hung it round his neck, ignoring the furious hissing of the cat. Now the noise in the hollow chimney sounded metallic and rasping, and there was an acrid smell in the room. He heaved himself to his feet, one hand on the crucifix, the other gripping the great poker and squared up to what was coming...

After reading the diary I checked out some facts. Newspaper cuttings from the local paper for early March 1933 reported that a body had been found in the sitting room of a cottage in New Street. There was evidence of a frantic struggle, and injuries to the body suggested a wild animal attack. There was no trace of an assailant, or any theft involved, and in view of the length of time between death and discovery, the cause remained a mystery.

I visited several shops in Hart Street where Uncle may have sought shelter, but so much had changed in eighty years that I found nothing like the shop he entered. So what to make of it all? I wondered. It seemed logical to infer that he suffered from delusions, which led to a breakdown of some kind. And he was ill and isolated, and after the death of his wife, probably clinically depressed.

So that ended my enquiries and soon afterwards Anne came home. Looking after her I forgot about Uncle's death, for she was either awake and in terrible pain, or more often in bed and delirious. Life became unbearable for me. She died one evening, as we were sitting together before the fireplace. I held her in my arms, and then she was gone. In a sense, of course, she had already died, but it didn't make my grief any less terrible.

Now I was on my own in the cottage and all was not well. I would sense things moving out of the corner of my eye: shapes flickering past, shadows too fast to focus on. And at night when the wind howled around the chimney I would lie awake, thinking of the past, of Uncle and Anne. I bought a dog. In fact I bought three, one after the other and kept none of them, for I found their incessant howling unnerving.

One evening, late in December, I was dozing in front of the fire when I sensed a movement in the room. Reaching for my glasses I turned towards the stairs where a huge cat with great, green eyes sat lashing its tail, its body stiff with tension. As I edged towards the hearth to grasp a poker, it sprang, but as it did so a dark shape leapt from the shadows, snatched it up in its jaws and both animals disappeared.

Did I imagine it? I must admit the possibility. But in the instant that I saw the cat's attacker I recognised it as the outline of a wolfhound which had once belonged to my wife's sister. Rufus adored Anne when they were both alive. And in death? Had she somehow sent him to help me in an hour of need?

Again it's possible, but unlikely. However, my experiences in the cottage were leading me to modify my views about Uncle's state of mind. Perhaps what he experienced weren't delusions after all. Was there something associated with the cottage that might be described as evil? But not at all like the kind of evil they said I'd committed when they found Anne's body in the sitting room. An "evil, brutal and frenzied attack", they said, when they arrested me. But what I did was not evil. Was wanting to kill the pain and set her free, evil? I held her in my arms and battered and crushed the dreadful thing to death. Did they think that was easy for me?

I got rather confused after they broke in, and found what they did, and they tell me I fought with them when they tried to take her body away. Since then, as you might expect, I've had many sessions with kind people to help straighten things out. Apparently the cat is a symbol of my repressed guilt about killing Anne, and Rufus represents her forgiveness. I always agree, of course, it makes them happy, and then they leave me alone.

But you know, it's not much of a life here in this place, and it makes me so angry. They don't know about my dreams, every night and always the same; when I see the beams and read the runes, and harken to what they have to say. And I know the terrible power and strength they bestow on we few who listen, and can understand them. I know what's in the well, and I know who was in the back room in the shop Uncle visited, so long ago. And if you've wondered if an underground passage connects the cellar in the shop in Hart Street to the well in New Street, I know the answer to that. And I know what has dwelt long ages in that dark place, waiting and waiting.

I know all these things, and they treat me as if I'm stupid. If only they knew my power they'd treat me better. But one day soon they'll find out how I feel, and what I can do. And when I've finished with them I'll be free. Free to track down others who, like you, know my story. Look forward to our meeting, I do! Think about that tonight in your cosy bed, when you hear the wind whistling, and hear a thump you can't explain. And the next night and the night after that. Feels good, doesn't it?

DISHONOUR
AMONGST THIEVES

You really wouldn't relish having to tell the formidable Jim Pendleton to cut short a well-earned vacation in the Bahamas. But the clients who'd sent for him didn't care about his feelings, and he knew better than to ignore their wishes. And so he went without delay to Valletta, the capital of Malta, that grim fortress, battered by centuries of military occupation.

There's an archway in the high city ramparts allowing access to the inner town, and in front of this entrance is a circular piazza with a baroque fountain. Here, amid piles of rubbish, half suffocated by diesel fumes, locals wait for the rural buses that constantly arrive and depart in a welter of clamour and pollution. Sheltered from all this by trees and a high wall is the Phoenician Hotel, and it was here that Jim was booked to stay.

The hotel was once grand, but only a few remnants of its stylish past still lingered on. The Imperial Bar was one, with its ancient ceiling fans murmuring away, cooling the patrons perched on their high bar stools. Heavy, embossed ashtrays containing olives rested on marble-topped tables, and an intense cedar-wood fragrance, culled from the smoke of countless cigars, impregnated the carpet and the mahogany woodwork. No ray of sunshine ever slanted into this low-lit shrine, and no street sound ruptured its muted, masculine calm.

Jim liked women, but preferred drinking with men, and so the Imperial Bar suited him down to the ground. The ladies avoided it like the plague, favouring the Bar Brasserie near the hotel's entrance for 'happy-hour' cocktails. They also eschewed the formal dining room where he always ate, with its potted palms, ancient waiters, crisp white tablecloths and tarnished silver service.

He sat and drank in the bar every night of his stay. Some people feel that drinking alone is sad, but the thought never occurred to him. He'd sit happily for hours under the whispering fans, swirling his whisky in the special cut-glass tumbler, quietly reserved for serious topers, listening to the pleasant tinkle of ice and passing the time of day with the barman, Frankie. He was a black American from the Deep South, and that's all Jim knew about him. That was how he liked it to be with bartenders. He held that if you started thinking of them as people with problems it would ruin the pleasure of drinking, and Scotch, mixed with a pinch of pity and a dram of drinker's guilt, wasn't his choice of cocktail.

In the daytime he'd hang around the hotel, waiting for a client to call. They never rang in the evening, so after dinner, he'd saunter round the inner town before returning to the hotel. Without the buses the piazza was deserted, and after crossing the square in front of the silent fountain he'd stroll through the archway in the ramparts, his footsteps sounding hard and hollow on the worn flagstones.

Beneath the looming walls it was gloomy, even in the day, and at night the streetlights, smeared with dead insects, emitted a feeble, yellow glow, giving the thin streets and narrow squares the illusion of a foggy night in Victorian London. Beyond the archway there was a small theatre, and one night Jim's eye was caught by a poster stuck on its front door proclaiming that a 'Magical Event', featuring a psychic performer, was replacing a scheduled programme. He noted it, shrugged and carried on walking.

Behind the theatre heavily worn steps led up to a narrow alleyway broadening out onto a rocky platform, with a fine view over the sea, and in the hush of the evening, when the sea breeze had cooled things down, Jim enjoyed looking across the water to the pretty villages of Vittoriosa and Senglea. The lights from the distant cafés danced and distorted in the moving waves, fishing boats moved silently out to sea, and often there was a cruise liner alongside the waterfront, its cabin lights gleaming beneath a string of bobbing, multi-coloured bulbs.

That evening, after he'd watched a ship disembark, Jim returned to the hotel as usual. Max the doorman, in his mustard-coloured, brass-buttoned uniform and top hat, opened the door and saluted. Jim always slipped people like him a generous something, for he never knew when he might need them, and he preferred getting a woman via a doorman rather than relying on his barman. Max gave every satisfaction in this respect, and was discreet and reliable.

Jim went across the lobby where a few guests were relaxing on sofas, and strolled across to the empty bar. "Right on schedule, Mr Jim," said Frankie, glancing up from the newspaper he was reading. Jim liked barmen to look the part, and Frankie was tall and slim, with shiny, slick-backed hair, pencil-thin moustache, a great smile, and a black tie when on duty. Like all good barmen he seemed to be a permanent feature, but in fact he hadn't been there very long.

"Evening, Francis," Jim nodded, easing himself onto his usual stool and downing the double Scotch Frankie had poured for him. "Any interesting guests?"

"An Italian conductor, with his 'daughter', for a series of concerts," said Frankie, polishing a glass. "A delegation from Chicago with a few Sicilians, playing big-time poker in the De Vere Suite, and a guy who contacts spirits. So they say."

"Really," said Jim, pushing his empty glass across the bar.

He recalled the psychic performer on the poster, but it hadn't intrigued him much then, and certainly didn't now. The spirits he valued were to be found in a glass, and he was only interested in an immediate future containing a fresh supply. Frankie started fixing his drink and, as he did so, glanced up, and whispered, "Talk of the devil," and Charles Elliott came into Jim's life.

Publicity images of older performers rely heavily on youthful shots and airbrushing, and the image of the psychic on the theatre poster fixed the viewer with an hypnotic stare that seemed unreal. But Charles's gaze really was mesmeric, his piercing eyes intensely blue, and full of light. Middle aged, clean shaven and slim, he spoke softly with a faint Canadian accent, and smiled readily. His well-cut linen suit was neatly pressed, there was a carefully arranged pink silk handkerchief in his top pocket, his bow tie was fashionably patterned, and his shoes were English and handmade.

They nodded to each other and Jim invited Charles to join him at the bar. He wasn't performing until the following evening, and so they had time to get acquainted. They were both widely travelled and past masters at sizing up strangers, and it didn't take them long to appreciate that they both lived off their wits. They didn't trust each other an inch, but liked each other's company and shared a love of whisky.

Charles had left British Columbia many years before in haste, and had been hurrying ever since. He'd tried farming, forestry, and prospecting, managed a casino, done time, and had been married umpteen times. But there was no hint of what had brought him to Malta, or led to his performing on the stage.

One afternoon Jim had secretly attended one of Charles's matinees, and saw how he fed back to his audiences clever inferences based on what they'd told him. It was skilfully done, assisted by the absolute command he'd established over them. No magic there then, but Jim couldn't help wondering why the lapdogs the ladies brought into the theatre howled so much when he appeared.

"Charles, how much of what you do is just working the audience?" Jim asked him one night.

"Most of it," Charles said, swirling the drink in his glass.

"And do you really have psychic powers? Hear voices or see things, that sort of thing?"

"Yes I do. Sometimes I get this strange feeling, like being drunk, and if I close my eyes I see moving images, but not clearly, more like objects distorted under running water. I can't explain when they're going to appear or why they come. And all my life I've wondered about the cause and effect of my insight."

"I don't understand."

"As I said, I see things others can't – like events that haven't yet taken place. But I don't know if what I see is going to occur anyway, or if what comes into my mind happens later."

"You mean you see into the future, and then it takes place, *because* you've thought of it?" said Jim.

"Yes, and that would mean influencing events, wouldn't it?" Charles said, bleakly.

"Difficult to prove or disprove. Do you always have to see the images to be able to see the future, and make predictions?"

"Not always," said Charles. "Let me concentrate for a moment, and I'll try to anticipate something which you'll think is highly unlikely but will happen tonight. I'll write down my prediction, Frankie can keep my note, and at twelve o'clock, we'll read what I've written."

He closed his eyes for a moment, and then scribbled something onto a scrap of paper which he gave to Frankie. He put it into a locked drawer under the bar and gave the key to Jim. As Charles stood up to go he whispered in Jim's ear, "Tonight you'll find a good home for the €200 you lifted from my luggage."

He was right. Soon after they'd met, whilst Charles was performing at a matinee, Jim had gone to his room, and inside one of his suitcases found a huge roll of euros. He pocketed a couple of hundred, but more out of habit than greed.

"No offence, Charles," said Jim. "Early days and only a token amount to cover our bar bill. Anyway, I found some of my things in your suitcase."

"Do you know why I took them?" Charles laughed. "So that you wouldn't feel too bad about lifting my money! And you had to leave them there or I'd have known you'd been through my things." He handed Jim back his jade cufflinks and some silver collar stiffeners, grinned, waved and left.

"Another whisky, Francis," said Jim, "and make it a bloody big one."

There was a pause and he glanced at Frankie, who looked down. "Pardon my saying so, Mr Jim," he said, "but your slate's been getting pretty big these days. Fact is, a little something would help me square the management."

"What the fuck is this, Frankie?" said Jim. "I'm going to push off without paying for my room, and settling my bar bill, is that what they think?"

"They had some non-payers, a while back," said Frankie miserably. "I told them you was okay. You always seen me right – what with the tips you gave me on the horses and, truth is, I put some of my winnings into your bar account to keep them quiet. But I sure could do with it now."

"How much do you need, Frankie?"

"Two hundred euros."

Jim fished out his wallet, and handed him two hundred and fifty. "Keep the change, Frankie, and don't worry, I'll pay what I owe when I leave."

Charles came back at midnight, and they read his note: "Frankie will ask you for two hundred euros tonight, and you'll give it to him." And he was spot on when he said Jim wouldn't have believed what he'd written. It happened all right and Jim couldn't deny or explain it, but that didn't mean he believed in a psychic explanation. But how, he wondered, did Charles know he'd rifle through his belongings? Now that was a mystery.

★ ★ ★

When Charles had several more days to go before his contract ended, he seemed uneasy, but loosened up after a few drinks. Jim always thought he'd spent as much energy concealing his past as he did foretelling the future, and now he sensed something serious was about to catch up with him. But if Jim was to help he'd need to know quickly, for he'd had word from his clients and things were on the move for him.

His professional dealings were complex and the only common thread running through them was their illegality. From time to time wealthy and influential people employed him to realise the value of their jewellery, works of art and antiques. These were so precious that only someone with the utmost credibility could be trusted to handle them, and produce the money the client expected. Delivery dates couldn't always be guaranteed, which was why he'd been kicking his heels in Valletta awaiting instructions. But now that he'd received them he'd be leaving the island – good news for him, but not for Charles if he needed his help.

"It's as bad as it gets," he said. "I've seen someone I don't want to meet checking in to the hotel, and I've got to get the hell out of here."

Jim took his arm and led him to a corner of the bar. "When I've finished this drink, I'm going down to the harbour to meet a boat just in from Palermo," he said. "It's delivering some things to me, then going straight back. I can get you on it – the harbourmaster's people can be squared, and you'll need a few hundred euros to pay the crew. When you get to Sicily, I'll arrange for you to lie up in Taormina and then you can fly from Catania, or get across to mainland Italy. But the boat won't wait a second longer than it has to, so just grab what you can't do without, and we'll go as soon as you're ready."

"I'll be back as soon as I can," said Charles. He returned in ten minutes carrying a small pigskin case and was in such haste that he forgot his mobile phone as he scrambled aboard the boat. He shook Jim's hand, gave him an intense look and said, "When you get back from Singapore, contact Frankie in London at the Connaught Hotel."

His words hardly registered with Jim, for he'd now received his long-awaited goods from Sicily. He'd no plans for going to Singapore, no idea why Charles had mentioned Frankie, and his mind was full of how he was going to broker the items from the boat. Back in his room he looked at the goods. They were tiny, ancient sculptures, rather battered and distressed, Persian perhaps or Mesopotamian. He had real experts to help him with articles like these, and often got more than his clients expected, creaming off the extra profit.

But when he checked his email everything changed, for he found an urgent summons from his most demanding clients, to go at once to Singapore. Everything else had to go on hold, and he reserved his hotel room in Malta, put the items from Sicily in his room safe, locked it and left the next morning.

★ ★ ★

Five days later he returned on a delayed flight, and all was quiet when he reached the hotel. Once in his room he unpacked, took out the items from Singapore, opened the safe and found that the goods from Sicily were gone.

After the first wave of panic he took stock. He couldn't put the word out, for the initial 'loss' of the items was well known in certain circles, and the last thing he wanted was his Sicilian clients getting wind of their disappearance. There was only one way out. His clients had no interest in how he raised the amount of money they'd specified, as long as their anonymity was preserved. There was a small fortune involved, but Jim reckoned he could buy time by financing it from his own resources. It would practically clean him out, but when he'd covered himself he'd track down the thieves, and they'd pay dearly when he caught them.

There was nothing for it but to leave for Europe and start raising the money. He managed to get a booking online for an early BA flight to London the next morning, and started packing. On leaving the hotel he asked the reception staff to pass on a generous tip to Frankie, only to find that he'd left the hotel, without notice, five days before. That was on the very morning when he'd left for the Far East. So could Frankie be connected with the theft of his goods?

On arriving in London, Jim checked in to the small hotel discreetly placed off Berkeley Square that he kept up his sleeve. From there he began raising money on the security of his properties, did some fancy footwork on various Swiss accounts and called in his debts. The money was shaping up, and when it arrived and he'd paid his clients he'd be broke, but still alive and with his reputation intact.

Nevertheless the theft left a sour taste in his mouth, and the lack of an explanation irked him even more. No con man likes to be played for a sucker, and the fate of the items needed solving. As a first step, Jim decided to follow up Charles's lead and contact Frankie at the Connaught Hotel. He left a message and his email address, and the next day received an email from Frankie telling him that although they couldn't meet, there would be a package waiting for him at reception, which he should pick up at once. When he collected the package the note inside said, "First-class return ticket enclosed for 19.05 train from Waterloo tonight. Enclosed key will open luggage locker 173, mainline station, Brighton. Room booked and paid for you at the Imperial Hotel, unlimited credit at the bar. When you leave, watch platform six."

That evening, as the train pulled out of the station, Jim spotted Frankie on the platform. But in the place of a barman was a Rasta with long locks, wearing a black leather jacket and distressed jeans. And with him was an all-American type, wearing a baseball hat, shorts and trainers. But the blue eyes were a giveaway. They waved and smiled, and Jim laughed and nodded in reply, looking back long after they'd disappeared from view.

Later that evening in the hotel bar in Brighton, he raised a glass to them. For in the hotel safe was the case from the station locker, containing the Sicilian goods, together with a £20,000 'gift' in cash, a first-class return ticket to the Bahamas and a hotel reservation. The attached note read: "Enjoy the rest of your holiday. Spend the money unwisely, and a fond farewell. Good knowing you, Jim." It signalled the end of their relationship, for when he rang Frankie at the Connaught, he'd left. The pair of them wanted closure, and that's exactly what they'd got.

But why return the items to him in London? Jim suspected that they'd planned to rob him and escape together, but when Charles panicked and took the boat he had no mobile and couldn't tell Frankie the deal was off. He assumed that was to thank him for his help in getting Charles away. But Frankie, unaware of their altered plans went ahead, took the items and then decamped to London, where he knew Jim would be headed.

So had Jim been rolled over by two skilled con men, on the make for whatever they could find, and well placed to find it in Malta? Unpalatable but likely. And what of Charles's psychic gifts? Jim suspected that he could guess he'd go through his luggage. As for the €200 loan business – maybe they just couldn't resist doing a scam like that! But how could Charles know that he'd be going to Singapore, when even Jim didn't know himself? And why was a hunted man performing on the stage for all the world to see? What was that all about?

Jim didn't think he'd ever find all the answers. But what he did know was how much he'd miss sitting in the faded grandeur of the Imperial Bar in the Phoenician Hotel and catching sight of Charles making his way to the bar. He could almost hear Frankie getting out the ice cubes to put into his thirty-year-old Ardmore, in his sparkling, cut-glass tumbler, then him inhaling the heady aroma, and feeling the drink slipping down, smooth as silk, warming and wonderful.

Who cares about what happened or what's going to happen, when you can hear that sound in your ears, and that taste in your throat? he thought. *And who cares that you can't rely on people you like?* Jim didn't feel betrayed by the pair, for that would imply a frustrated expectation of trust, and no such understanding existed between them. In any case, he knew that trust, although a beautiful thing like a flawless diamond, was just as rare. And so his toast to them was: "To all we travellers, outcasts and misfits, who neither give nor expect trust, ones without illusions, destined to live fully and die alone."

Now all Jim wanted to do was resume his holiday in the Bahamas, but even that was not to be. There were no survivors from the crash on his booked flight. And so he would not live to finish his holiday, broker his goods or live to enjoy the rewards. But nor would he discover that his Sicilian goods had been replaced by fakes, or that the money 'gift' was in counterfeit notes. So much for any hint of friendship or thanks, you might say. But if Charles could foresee what was going to happen to Jim, it would surely be a waste not to keep his illicit goods. And why not give him a gift of cash, out of friendship, to make him happy, even if he would never spend it?

Was Charles really cursed with the gift of future vision? And was he tortured by the thought that he might be creating the future from a thought or a wish? And did that mean he had a hand in Jim's death? No one will ever know. Perhaps Charles was a tragic Flying Dutchman, forever destined to be alone, tortured by his gift, and so different from his fellow men. And if he was, would he have traded what we have to settle for, people like us, living out our days in profound ignorance of what's to come? Would he have settled for that? Would you?

THE FLAT

I t was nine o'clock on a Saturday evening, and to Mark Hanson, dozing on the sofa, the gentle but unexpected knock sounded like a thunderclap. Few would have sensed anything over the sound of the television, even with the volume turned down, and fewer still with what he'd had to drink, but he was instantly alert, his reflexes always highly tuned when he was on an assignment.

But who would knock? Certainly not a burglar. An opportunist intruder? Unlikely given the mansion block's effective security system. Someone from another flat, then? But when he'd checked he'd found that the ground-floor flat was being redecorated, and the first-floor was empty and up for sale. And at 2000 hours, the girl in the top apartment had driven away in her silver Audi.

He'd been tailed, hadn't he? He gripped his fists so hard that the nails dug into his palms. Oh God, oh God, what was he doing here? Doing time that was what. For drinking himself senseless every day, not holding down a proper job and falling in with the wrong people. Not doing any damn thing right. And this time the sentence wouldn't have any remission for good conduct, it would just go on and on and on.

Through the welter of self-pity he felt a stab of fear. Had he got something wrong? In his mind he went back over his instructions. He was to arrive at 1900 hours and wait for someone to let themselves in to the flat using their key. No need for them to knock on the door. Then, after he'd given them the password 'deadfall', he was to hand over the briefcase. The briefcase! Where was it? Think, think! He got so muddled these days. Looking down, he saw it by the side of the sofa. Now, what else? He was to leave the sealed letter he'd been given in the drinks cupboard. Yes, he'd done that, but wasn't there more? Identifying people, something like that? Or had he got that mixed up with another job? Then he remembered the knock.

He heaved himself up and made for the door, his stockinged foot knocking over and crushing the half-filled wine glass he'd left on the floor. The heavy claret spilled into the ashtray on the floor which overflowed, mixing the wine with black ash and cigarette butts. A dark stain spread over the deep pile of the light-coloured carpet, mingling obscenely with the blood from his cut foot. He regarded the mess with revulsion and despair. Another fucking mess, his life was full of them.

He pulled splinters of glass from his foot, and when he reached the door he listened, pressing his ear to the wood. Nothing. He looked at the locks, noting that one was a Yale and the other old fashioned with the key still in the escutcheon. He twisted the Yale, releasing the locking lever, gently turned the older key and opened the door a fraction. He held his breath but sensed only the throb of his foot and a pulse in his temple. As he eased the door open his body tensed to take the impact of a sudden onrush, but nothing happened, and when he peered out he saw that the corridor was empty. There was an outside wall with a door leading to a fire escape ten metres to his right, and to his left the stairs wound down two flights to the entrance hall, and one up to the flat above.

He crept to the fire-escape door and pressed the bar. The door opened with a jerk and a gust of night air hit him in the face. Down below, visible through the iron lattice of the steps, he saw wet pavements, shining in the glow of street-lights. A lone figure was walking along the opposite side of the road, bordering the park, and beyond he could make out the bare branches of trees by the river, outlined against the glow of West End lights.

He closed the door and the over-heated air in the hall seemed to swallow up the chill and noise from outside. There was the sweetish smell of emulsion paint left over from the redecoration of the ground-floor flat, but apart from that the building was lifeless and dead. He crept back along the corridor and leaning over the banisters looked down, his eyes following the curve of the stairs winding around to the empty reception area below. He limped back to the flat, leaving blood from his foot on the carpet, and once inside stood undecided. Then he went to the drinks cabinet, poured himself a large glass of wine and drank it quickly. Emboldened, he decided to check out the building on the ground floor.

Putting on his shoes and coat he left the flat, closing the door with care and making sure the Yale lock was not engaged. He hurried downstairs and quickly inspected the entrance lobby, checking that the doors and windows were secure. He peered outside through the darkened windows, shading the light from behind him with his hand, but saw nothing. After limping up the stairs he tried to re-enter the flat using the key of the Yale, but something was wrong – the lock seemed jammed. He swore, fiddled with the key, pushed the door hard, but it remained firm. And then it dawned on him that it was locked!

A moment of shock and disbelief and then anger took over. He was furious with the situation but most of all with himself. He didn't know what to do next. But his intuition told him that someone was inside the flat – there was no time for them to have gained access from outside without him seeing or hearing them. That also meant that they'd been there for some time. So what the hell was going on?

What could he do? Force his way back into the flat and confront whoever he found inside? He was too experienced and not drunk enough to fall for that one. He'd be caught in the wrong place doing the wrong thing, and then he'd be punished, and he'd had quite enough of that. Oh, just to walk away from it all, and start again. In his dreams! He needed time to think. Maybe a walk in the cold would do the trick. And a drink, he must have a drink.

Hanson went down the stairs, out through the entrance doors and turned left along the deserted road. After a few minutes the road veered away to his right towards the river, and he could make out the shape of a bridge. There were cold lights on the opposite bank, but what interested him more were the warm, welcoming ones of the Rising Sun pub over the road.

He crossed, entered the crowded saloon and pushed his way to the bar where Len Finch, the thick-set publican, was polishing glasses. He ordered a double whisky, which he downed in one. The rush of fiery liquid gave him a boost, and he ordered another.

"Raw night," said Len, passing the whisky over. "Gets the customers in, though. If you can't get a full house on a Saturday night in November you're in the wrong job."

He scanned the people in the bar. *Usual mix*, he thought. Regulars from the old GLC housing estate over the river, playing darts. They seldom drank on the Chelsea side of the Thames, whose pubs were full of Americans in summer, drinking half-pints of warm beer, and telling themselves they were enjoying it. Over in the corner he saw the usual group of anoraks who had adopted the pub over the last few months, whilst in the snug, some trendy youngsters were getting into the mood before moving on to a party. A few office security guards coming on or going off duty were downing their last pints by the bar and, as usual, there was a loner, like this fellow. 'Drifters', he called them. He'd seen them come and he'd seen them go – in from who knows where, a few drinks and then away into the night. And for all he knew, into the river. Funny to think that this warm, friendly bar might be the last place on earth they saw before plunging into its cold, dark waters.

Hanson stared down into his glass, whilst Len polished more glasses and speculated about him. Tall, slim, well-dressed, educated voice, clipped and polite, but slurred. Officer type, but not putting it on like some did, and a bit pissed and anxious. Extra-marital issues, most like, was Len's take on the man.

The drink relaxed Hanson until he remembered the briefcase. He nearly fainted with shock, but recovered enough to pull up the collar of his coat, give Len a nod of thanks and make his way to the door. *Another one for the river*, wondered the publican, but he'd never know. Downstream there was no way of telling where someone had gone in, for the current was swift, the night was dark, nobody was around and a body would be swept down to Deptford in no time. He put down his drying-up cloth, and went to chat to the security men, patting the backside of his buxom Australian barmaid on the way. He liked women to have a bit of bulk, like Olga upstairs, his Russian girlfriend.

After the warmth of the pub, the cold night air gave Hanson a shock. In the bar he'd half resolved not to return to the flat, but that was before he'd remembered the briefcase. Dear God, what choice did he have? He noticed that the night was cloudless with the moon bright in a dark sky, a few stars glittered and gusts of icy wind blew fitfully from the river. It was not a night to have to cope with trouble, fuelled as he was by booze, guilt and fear.

He pulled his covert coat tightly round his shoulders. Best foot forward, Hanson! His footsteps rang on the damp pavement.

There was a black Porsche parked in the road near the block of flats and he clocked the number plate. Even with Scotch and wine swilling around inside him, he had perfect recall for numbers. It had always been like that with him. Not helpful, though, if you were being interrogated and wanted to forget things. When he reached the block he glanced up at the dark windows and then scanned the road. No one was around, and the bare branches in the street trees twitched and scraped together in the gusty wind. *How desolate London streets could be*, he thought.

The entrance to the mansion block had double doors with glass panels and was protected by a security lock with a metal keypad. Recalling the combination he'd been given on a slip of paper, he opened the door, stepped inside and listened. After the bitter wind, the silence inside the lobby was heavy and charged with menace, and only overwhelming fear induced him to climb the stairs. He paused outside the flat for a moment and tried the Yale key. It turned easily, and after pushing open the door a fraction, he peered through the narrow gap. Seeing nothing he stepped inside.

The curtains were still drawn, the ugly stain was on the carpet, and the briefcase was unopened, and still where he'd left it. Thank God. Limping across to the window, he gently moved the curtain and looked down. Seeing nothing unusual in the street below, he turned and looked around the room.

The ceiling was high with elaborate moulding around the cornices, and the walls were covered with old-fashioned patterned wallpaper, blotched and discoloured. Heavy, faded curtains framed the windows facing the road, and the sofa, chairs and tables, scratched and soiled, were solid, Victorian and continental. The carpet was thick and badly scuffed, and the whole flat smelt of chalky dust, cheap polish, stale cooking and neglect. *God*, he thought, *another barren place.*

Hanson felt a strong urge for drink. On a sideboard were empty decanters for whisky, brandy and sherry, but he'd found full bottles of claret and Scotch in the drawers below. He poured himself a large whisky, drank it in one and instantly felt better. He decided to check out the other rooms. There was a passage from the sitting room to the bathroom and leading from it were three doors. The first led to a kitchen with a stained sink and gently dripping tap, an ancient fridge with a large, tarnished chrome handle, some pine cupboards and a wooden table covered with a greasy, plastic cloth. He looked into the fridge and opened several drawers but found nothing. No food or used plates, no cutlery, no scraps in the bin.

He returned to the hall and paused outside one of the other rooms. There was no sound from within and opening the door, he wryly reflected how much of his evening had been spent on opening and closing doors, not to mention running between them. The room was a bedroom with a dirty, ill-fitting cream carpet, dusty Venetian blinds, a double bed with a French headboard and a chipped reproduction Louis 15th-style dressing table.

On the bed a man was lying on his back, as if sleeping. Hanson felt the pulse on the neck and wrist, confirming what he already knew: the man was dead. But there was no obvious cause of death, no wounds or signs of a struggle, no pills on the table or weapons of any kind. He was wearing an army officer's uniform, without buttons, badges or labels, and the shoes, still on his feet, were unremarkable brown Oxfords. And his pockets were quite empty.

An alarm bell was ringing in Hanson's ears, and it was warning him of something called a 'set-up'. Get him here, make sure there was booze around to get him nicely relaxed, and there'd be lots of his fingerprints around the flat, including some on the body. Maybe they were still arranging it when he arrived, and his falling asleep on the sofa would have been a bonus for them. But someone had made a noise that he thought was a knock on the door, and he'd woken up. And when he'd left the flat, they'd locked him out to finish the job, knowing that he'd be back for the briefcase.

He returned to the sitting room, poured himself a large whisky, sat down on the sofa and wondered what to do. Part of him was exhausted and terrified, and another part couldn't give a damn. Checking out the third room delayed making a decision and so, drink in hand, he went down the corridor and casually pushed open the door to the room. He should have known better, for a bulky, bearded man hurled himself out of the room.

Hanson fell over backwards, grabbing at the flying figure, largely to regain his balance, but the man, twisting to his left, punched him hard in the stomach and, as Hanson fell to his knees, ran into the sitting room and grabbed the briefcase from the floor. Then he wrenched open the flat door and rushed down the stairs and across the lobby, slamming the front doors behind him.

Racked with spasms of retching, Hanson lay on his back, the stench of vomit in his nostrils, and wept. He wept for what he'd lost, for what he'd become, and for what might have been. And he wept because he'd reached the end of the road, and he had neither the strength nor the will to go on.

★ ★ ★

By now it was getting on for midnight. The last revellers from the Rising Sun were making their way home, but only the lone group of anoraks hung around chatting near the pub entrance. Most of the others made for the river, and over the bridge they went, wrapped up against the cold, with the wind tearing through the exposed ironwork, and the current pounding the concrete piers. The lights on the bridge showed the swollen waters racing away downstream, shining and sinuous, until they were lost in the darkness.

A white Mercedes was parked at the side of the road leading to the bridge. In the driving seat Susan Standish was sipping coffee from a thermos, which was now nearly empty. The locals passed by, heads bowed against the wind, chattering and swearing cheerfully, until the sound of their joking and laughter died away, and she was alone again.

Susan first saw him as he walked slowly over the bridge, hunched and unsteady, clearly the worst for wear. He stopped at the highest point of the bridge, held on to the parapet of the bridge with both hands, and gazed down into the churning floodwaters. She put down her coffee, got out of the car and walked towards him. He showed no sign of being aware of her as she approached.

"Do you know one of the oddest things about people who throw themselves from bridges?" she asked.

Hanson started and turned, focussing unsteadily on her. "What?" he said. "What did you say?"

"I said, 'What's odd about people who throw themselves from bridges?'"

"People, bridges…" he glared at her. "I don't give a fuck about them. Who the hell are you?"

"They take their shoes off," she said. "Don't you think that's odd?"

"Why should I care?" Hanson turned back to look down at the river.

"Because you're here on a bridge and maybe thinking about taking off your shoes."

"Why should you care? Mind your own fucking business." He turned angrily towards her, his legs buckled under him, and he sank to his knees.

She grasped his coat lapels to help cushion his fall, his body slumped forwards and holding his head between her hands she laid it gently against the stonework. Looking over the bridge she saw the group clustered around the pub entrance and stood up waving towards them. They could see quite plainly what was happening, but they instantly stopped talking and rapidly melted away into the night.

Len Finch from the Rising Sun pub was starting to cross the bridge as Hanson collapsed. After his last customers had gone and he'd checked that the barmaid was clearing up properly, he'd take his terrier Nipper for a walk. It never varied – over the bridge, along the embankment and then back to the pub. He saw what was happening out of the corner of his eye and recalled that the last time he'd seen something like that he'd walked on, and the woman had jumped from the bridge. Bad business that. He crossed the road, pulling the dog behind him.

"You all right there?" he asked. Nipper sniffed around the fallen man, and Len gave a sharp jerk on his lead.

Susan, who was on her knees leaning over Hanson, turned and looked up at the bulky figure of Len. He was wearing a worn anorak and a brightly coloured woollen hat pulled down over his ears. "He's passed out," she said. "I'll need help getting him into my car." She gestured towards the Mercedes. "Can you give me a hand?"

"Friend of yours?" asked Len, without moving. He could swear he'd seen her around before but couldn't place where. Maybe waiting in her car. That meant one thing to Len, but close up she seemed too posh – and well dressed – to be a tart, and didn't speak like one either. Good looking, though.

"No, I was passing and saw him collapse. There's a first aid kit in the car, but I don't think he'll need it – he's just had too much to drink."

Like hell, you were passing, thought Len. "So where are you going to take him?" he said.

"I want to get him out of the cold, and see if he's got any identification on him."

"He was drinking in my pub earlier tonight, " said Len."The Rising Sun, just over the bridge."

"Yes, I know it," she said. "Help me to move him, will you? Keep him steady for a moment and I'll go and open the car door."

"Make it quick, then, I haven't got all night."

Susan ran to the car, opened the passenger door and hurried back to where Len, smoking a cigarette, was supporting the man. Nipper was whining and straining at his lead, and with a curse the publican reached across and released him from his lead. The dog scuttled off into the night.

"It'll be easier if we each take an arm, and lift together," Susan said.

Len grunted, and threw his cigarette over the parapet, the tip tracing a glowing arc as it disappeared into the darkness. "Should have called the police," he said.

Hanson's dead-weight took them by surprise. Half lifting and half dragging his body to the car, they manoeuvred him into the passenger seat. The publican straightened up, winced and massaged his back while Susan took Hanson's pulse. Len looked down at the body lolling in the passenger seat in the car, and glimpsed something round and metallic beneath the driver's seat.

"I'll see if he's got anything on him that might help us get him home," he said.

"No, no. Don't bother," said Susan hastily, "I can manage now."

But Len had already rummaged in the pocket of Hanson's coat and found a scrap of paper on which was an address, a combination lock number, and some keys. "I know where this is," he said, holding up the paper, and studying it in the light of a street lamp. "One of the flats in a mansion block by the park. Not far, but too far for him." He handed the items to Susan. "Let's just get him there, and then we can all get some sleep. Some of us have got work to do in the morning." He gazed up and down the road, swinging Nipper's lead. "Do you know this bloke?" he asked, kicking at some imaginary stone on the road. "You weren't just passing by, I saw you waiting for something or someone. Was it for him?"

Susan flushed with anger, "Even if I *was* waiting for someone it's none of your business," she snapped, "but I still need your help if we're to get him home. I'm not leaving him here all night."

"All right," he said, hurriedly. "Keep your hair on. I'll help you get him to that address, but that's all. You drive and I'll follow. There's not enough room in the car for all of us, and you've got the address I've given you."

Susan drove away from the bridge, followed the road bending away from the river and stopped opposite an Edwardian mansion, converted into apartments. She glanced up at the windows, noting that the ones on the second floor had curtains pulled across, but all the others had the blank look of empty flats.

Len arrived, breathing heavily and leaned on the car, looking down at Susan. She gave him the paper with the combination for the front door, the keys he'd found in Hanson's pocket, and watched him as he climbed the steps to the entrance.

People who took Len at face value often saw him as basic and dull, but he'd been a regular soldier, ending up as a senior warrant officer in a good regiment. And as he approached the entrance he knew Hanson didn't live there. *You might need a note of the combination to get into your block if you were stupid and forgetful,* he thought, *but why would you need a note of your own address?* Maybe a friend had lent him the place, and maybe not. Maybe the woman had been waiting for him and maybe not. And maybe what he'd glimpsed under the seat of her car was for her own protection. And then again... The number worked for the security keypad and he pushed the door open, turned and gave her the thumbs up sign.

"Excellent," she called out to him and smiled. Len grinned back, thinking what a sucker he was for a pretty face. He returned to the Mercedes, and helped Susan heave Hanson out of the passenger seat. He grasped him under the arms, she took his legs, and together they struggled up the steps and into the lobby, where they propped him up on a chair near the front doors. They paused for breath. It was utterly silent and Susan looked up at the stairs leading to the apartments whose windows she'd seen from the road. "His flat's up there, on the second floor," she whispered to Len. "Let's get him inside."

They heaved Hanson up the stairs and when they reached the flat Susan knocked on the door, but there was no response. Len gave her Hanson's keys and she used the Yale to open the door. They carried him into the flat, laid him on the sofa, stood up and smiled across at each other.

"Well, what have we here?"

The voice was quiet, the delivery a languid drawl, but it was enough to make them both freeze. Susan turned towards the elegant, silver-haired speaker and opened her mouth to speak.

"Well, what we have here?" continued the man, looking at Hanson and ignoring her. "Is it someone who used to be the property of Her Majesty's Armed Forces? Or is all that really in the past? One never knows with people like him."

He turned to Susan. "And helping our hero to bed we have, shall we say, a former 'advisor' to those shining ones who ensure we all sleep soundly in our beds. 'Former' would be accurate, I think, Dr Standish. And that, I fear, is as far as my knowledge of the present company goes," he concluded silkily, turning to a large, sandy-haired man who had joined them from another room. "Can you furnish any more details of their companion, Chief Superintendent Palmer?"

"Leonard Finch, sometime RSO in Her Majesty's Irish Guards, former detective sergeant in the Met, and landlord of the Rising Sun public house for the past six years," said the man, grinning at Len.

"Well now, here we go again," said the elegant speaker. "That 'former' word keeps coming up, doesn't it? So what brings you three together in a place like this, with a body lying in the next room?"

"Who the hell are you?" demanded Len. "How come you know so much about us? And what's all this about a stiff?"

"Ah, Mr Finch – allow me to pose the questions. Our names would mean nothing to you. All you need to know is that we'll be having a nice chat later on, to get to know one other rather better, and that this gentleman will be taking notes." He looked at Hanson slumped on the sofa. "However, I don't think all of us will be up to such a discussion just now. We really must find the ex-major somewhere to rest and recover his wits."

He murmured something to his companion and then, turning to Susan and Len, said, "By nine o'clock tomorrow morning forensics will have finished here, and I'll want you here at ten in the morning, the pair of you. You can go now, but don't even think of running away." He gave a brief nod to his colleague who opened the door and gestured for them to leave.

In the corridor Len turned to Susan. "I don't know how far away you live," he said, "and it's not the Ritz, but there's a bed in the pub if you could use it."

"That makes sense," she said briskly. "Anything to get this thing sorted out as soon as possible. God, I could do with a drink!"

He nodded and together they left the flat, went down the stairs and climbed into her car. When they reached the pub, Len pointed out a narrow drive to the left of the building leading to a row of lock-up garages. Susan drove the SLK along the alleyway, and when she stopped the car Len jumped out and swung one of the garage doors upwards. Driving into the tight space, she squeezed out of the driver's seat, opened the boot and took out two bags.

"I always travel with a medical case," she said, when Len looked at her luggage. "There's a change of clothes in the other."

He unlocked a gate set in a high wooden fence protected by coils of razor wire, and taking one of her cases led the way to the back door of the pub, leading to a kitchen. At the far end of the room was a staircase, with a soiled patterned carpet, and when they reached the landing at the top of the stairs Len pointed to a door on the right and whispered, "You can use that room. If you still want that nightcap, turn right at the bottom of the stairs and the bar's in front of you. I'll join you there in a few minutes. Have a shower if you want, but quietly please – there are other people here." She nodded and he disappeared into a room at the far end of the corridor.

Fifteen minutes later Susan was sitting in the cold, cheerless bar, still smelling of stale beer, cigarettes and heated bodies. Fresh from her tepid shower she was enjoying a brandy and Len, tired and grey faced, was drinking a pint.

"Let me explain about tonight," Susan said, pausing whilst she drank some more brandy. "I was a doctor in the Army Medical Corps, and I treated soldiers who'd been wounded in Desert Storm. The first Gulf War took a lot of people by surprise – some of the weapons used were experimental, and many involved had little experience of fighting. Several of my patients suffered from severe combat trauma and stress."

Len took a pull at his pint, and sat upright. Somehow he'd morphed from being the publican of a dodgy pub into something more weighty.

Susan continued. "I became close to someone damaged in the war, and when he was invalided out of the army, I thought he might recover. But I was wrong. One night he walked alone to a bridge and disappeared. And so, from time to time I wait around on other bridges to see if I can help someone like Mike."

"Maybe tonight you did just that," said Len, "but I don't want to think about it or discuss it now, if you don't mind." *Or hang around here listening to any more of your lies*, he thought.

"I agree – let's wrap it up for tonight," she said, briskly, finishing her drink. They left the bar and parted at the top of the stairs. "I'll give you a call at eight," Len whispered and disappeared into the darkness. As she closed her door Susan heard a female voice, and a muttered response from Len. Lifting her medical bag onto the bed, she removed some items which she tucked into a small backpack, then kicked off her shoes, undressed, and got into bed. It was one o'clock, and after a while she dozed off.

She seemed to have been asleep for only a few minutes before she was jerked awake by a knock on the door. For a moment she'd no idea where she was, but when she remembered she felt drained and stale. The door opened, the ceiling light was switched on, and Len was looking at her from the door. Her watch said 1.45am.

"We must get back to the flat," he said, in a whisper. "Don't ask any questions, just do as I say. Be downstairs in five minutes." Then he was gone.

She swung her legs out of bed feeling the lino under her bare feet, cold and clammy. Could one ever feel clean in a room like this? In the corner of the room, behind a black, mildewed sheet of plastic was a cubicle, smelling of pine and rubber. She splashed some of the water onto her face from the meagre, icy trickle coming from the tap, put on a pair of jeans and a thick sweater, and picked up her backpack. Len was waiting in the bar when she got down.

"What's going on?" she asked.

"I didn't realise at first, but I know who they are, and they're not what they seem to be. Our drunken friend's going to be in a heap of trouble if we don't get back and help him."

"But what can we do?" she whispered.

"You don't survive in the army for thirty years, or the part of the Met I was in, without being able to look after yourself," he said. "And they can't have got up to much mischief since we left." He patted a bulky object in his pocket.

"Is that really necessary?" she asked.

"We're not dealing with nice people here," said Len. "Trust me."

It was nearly three o'clock and bitingly cold, but he insisted that they walk back to the apartment. They entered the building, climbed the stairs and outside the flat paused and listened. Hearing nothing, Len opened the door using Hanson's key. The living room was empty, there was no one in the kitchen and in the bedroom a body was lying on the bed. But this time it was Hanson's, and as they moved to the bedroom to examine him they heard a click as the Yale lock on the door closed behind them.

Shocked, they returned to the living room, where they found Palmer in front of the door, and the elegant speaker standing by the window, one hand still on the curtain, which he had pulled slightly aside. He turned and smiled across at them. "So the penny dropped, Mr Finch." It was the familiar, suave voice, but now with a very different tone. "We wondered if it would. What a pity. And that's in short supply around here, as you'll find out, very soon."

"Be careful, Dauncey, he's armed," said Susan, quietly, and Len spun round to face her, his eyes wide with anger and astonishment. Palmer, moving quickly for such a big man, pointed a gun at his head, and the publican scowled as the policeman frisked him and took the gun from his pocket.

"Who are you, bitch?" he said to Susan, and Palmer hit him hard in the mouth with the handle of his pistol. Len fell onto the sofa and wiped his bloodied mouth with the back of his hand.

Palmer let him recover and then, with a smile hit him again, knocking out a tooth that flew from his mouth in a jet of blood.

Susan turned to face Dauncey, her face white with fury. "What the hell are you doing here?" she rasped, and pointed at Palmer. "Bloody Special Branch! Who authorised him to meddle in things that don't concern him? If it's Hanson you're after, he's here because we need him here. And it's got nothing to do with your damned department or this flatfoot!"

"Ah, Hanson, to be sure. Not, I fear, the most *sober* of souls," Dauncey replied, smiling sourly. "But perhaps he's useful to you. Yes, I really think he is, but I do so wonder why."

"So he drinks. Wouldn't you if you'd been through what he has? When your lot left him to carry the can. An Iranian prison, wasn't it?"

"None of our doing, I do assure you, Susan." Dauncey turned to Palmer. "Perhaps Special Branch know?" Palmer, who was sitting in an armchair, looked up and gave a grin. He continued wiping Len's blood off the handle of his pistol.

"Like hell it was." Susan was really angry. "And don't think you've heard the end of this. Four months' surveillance of that damned pub with our boys on expenses, disguised like bloody ramblers. And on the very night we'd planned the snatch operation, there's this total fuck-up. Squads all over the country, just waiting for the word that we've got the top villains before they move in, and what happens?"

Dauncey shrugged, and Palmer, who'd finished cleaning his gun, grinned again, and stood up as Susan pointed to Len: "So he's walking his bloody dog and outside the pub, my boys are just waiting for my signal to take him and the terrorist thugs he's been harbouring. We've arranged for Hanson to be here in this damned flat, to start the interrogations and, hey presto, there he is, on the bridge pissed, witless and suicidal!"

For the briefest of moments, Dauncey betrayed the hint of an emotion: it could have been pity, remorse or contempt. "Hardly something to lay at our door, Susan."

Len, whose face had already swollen, livid with bruising, moved restlessly, and Palmer raised his pistol. Dauncey shook his head.

"And then I'm the meat in the bloody sandwich." said Susan.

"Don't *quite* follow you there," Dauncey moved over to the drinks cupboard, found a glass, wiped it tenderly with a spotless handkerchief and poured himself a small Scotch. He made a great fuss of finding some soda, carefully measured it into his drink and looked across to Susan, his eyebrows raised.

"Well, think about it – I'm between keeping Hanson from taking the plunge in the Thames and Len, who I can't arrest on his own, without his chums seeing what's going on, and disappearing for ever out of the back door of his bloody pub," Susan almost shouted in exasperation. "So what can I do? I wave my boys away, they pass on the glad tidings to HQ and all our agents are stood down! Thousands of hours of surveillance and millions of pounds just thrown away. Not to mention dozens of terrorist cells still going about their fucking murderous business, and all because one of your clowns, lurking about in this flat, runs out like a headless chicken, thumping Hanson on the way. Anyway what *are* you doing here?"

"My dear Doctor Standish, firstly I don't know who it was who Hanson surprised; and secondly, I'll let you into a little secret – you're not the only ones with an interest in the galloping major."

Susan suddenly looked weary and drained. "Don't tell me you tailed him to the flat!"

"Had a tip off, my dear Susan. Hanson was acting as someone's messenger boy as well as working for you, and he was delivering something to someone we needed to get our hands on very much indeed. Someone we're dying to meet, for an intimate little *tête-à-tête*. But when we turn up, this unknown idiot comes flying out of the mansion, and we hang around, Palmer and I, to see what else might happen. And out of the woodwork comes Hanson, clutching his stomach, and reeling all over the place.

172

Next thing we see is you ministering to him with Lennie here, and can't believe our eyes. And when you brought him back to the flat we hurried to welcome you home. Had to pretend we hadn't met, of course, for little Len's benefit."

"Quite a coincidence both of us being here at the same time, don't you think?" said Susan, frowning and massaging her temples.

Len, leaning back on the sofa and stemming the blood from his mouth with a handkerchief began a fit of coughing. Everyone ignored him as Dauncey continued.

"When the chief superintendent here claps eyes on our Len, he knows a lot of nasty things about him. But had Lennie clocked *him*? We take a gamble that he hasn't. No such luck! So the little bugger gets his little gun and has returned to polish us off. And you're invited too, Susan, he doesn't like witnesses, doesn't our Len. What a nasty piece of work. Hit him again, Palmer, if you think it'll help his coughing."

Palmer grasped Len's anorak, pulled him upright, hit him again hard in the mouth, and then pushed him back onto the sofa, retching blood.

Dauncey took off his half-moon spectacles, which he carefully wiped and gently replaced. "Of course, we knew about 'Operation Rising Sun'," he said. "But your masters didn't give ours the exact details of tonight's operation. How remiss and how regrettable, too – particularly for the young hero Hanson. 'Former hero', I suppose I should say."

"Yes, that's exactly what your lot like, isn't it? Everything tidy. At least we look after our people, when things don't work out."

Dauncey dropped his languid manner, just for an instant, but enough to reveal his dark side, rarely on show, and never to be ignored when it was.

"Oh, come off it, Susan, darling. You know you wouldn't get the convictions you want for your Rising Sun prosecutions if Hanson didn't spill more beans than he has already. The really tasty ones, from his infiltrating the Iranians, before they got him.

And if you don't get successful prosecutions for all the fish in your net, you get no thanks from the cousins on the Hill, the Mandarins or their slimy select committees. And boy, do you want that! And need it, even more."

"No more than you do with your turned agents and lousy networks in tatters," Susan spat at him.

Dauncey was undeterred. "Of course, of course – it all makes sense. You want Hanson to do a good job with who you scoop up from the pub, and just to make sure he does, you plant a corpse on him, with his fingerprints all over it, and threaten to lock him up for good unless he brings home the bacon. He'd like being in prison again, you bet. And when the terrorists get sent down for thirty years, you sit back, listen to all the applause and next stop the Queen's Birthday Honours list. Who thinks these things up?"

"Mark Hanson would have come up with the goods anyway, when he knew what the stakes were."

Dauncey paused, before continuing. "Yes, we thought about that: the 'Faithful Patriot Theory'. But then we got word he was working for someone else as well as us. Someone who knew about both of our departments and someone who didn't want your little scheme to work tonight. Hence our tip-off. They knew if we'd found Hanson with his package for delivery and the recipient, we'd have spirited them away. And that would have meant no identity parade for you, or Hanson being compromised with his dabs all over your planted corpse. So who might this other party be? The one really pulling the strings? The bloody IRA for all I know."

"Just shut up, Dauncey," shouted Susan. "That's your paranoia talking."

"Jesus Christ!" shouted Len, his voice sounding strange with his damaged mouth. "What are you two fucking *talking* about." Palmer raised his pistol but Dauncey again shook his head. "It's not bloody le Carré cold war gents we're dealing with here," shouted Len. "You just don't get it, do you? Do you know what 'deep cover' really means? How long was Hanson in that prison? Six months? How long have I been getting the trust of these terrorist thugs? Six fucking years. And you're about to blow that sky-high with your pathetic 'Operation Rising Sun'. Why didn't they leave it to us grown-ups in the SAS? And, by the way, I *do* know who's really pulling the strings."

"Bluff!" snapped Dauncey. "You're a bloody terrorist bastard. Kill him, Palmer, now."

There was a shocked silence in the room as the initiative shifted from Len to Palmer, and for a crucial instant he froze. Len grabbed his gun and shot him at point blank range in the head. Dauncey, diving behind the sofa and splattered with Palmer's blood, took a shot in mid-air that blew the side of his face clean away. Susan, bringing up her own pistol to fire, seemed to fly over backwards, as two bullets hit her in the chest, her gun flying high into the air and skidding away towards the door. Before it came to rest she was quite dead.

Len breathed deeply and looked around him. Blood dripped like oil from the furniture, soaking into the carpet already matted with red, while shredded flesh and brain tissue slid silently down the walls. The room, deathly quiet now, looked like an abattoir. He dragged the bodies onto the sofa where they sprawled ungainly in death, and began searching their clothing. When he reached Susan he remembered her pistol and glanced towards the door. There was nothing there. Very carefully, with Palmer's gun in his hand, he crept towards the bedroom. Not a man to take chances, Len Finch, but even he was surprised by the speed of Hanson from behind the door, as he blew his face and the back of his head off with the missing pistol.

★ ★ ★

It was very early that Monday morning when the girl with the silver Audi from the top flat came back. She stood for a moment inside the foyer, and then carried her small suitcase upstairs, past the doors of the other flats and entered her own apartment. For a moment she leant back on the closed door and smiled. In a moment she'd go to the flat below, and check if the courier who'd brought the briefcase had left a message for her in the arranged place. It was one of the last pieces in a complex jigsaw that Britain would never forget or be able to forgive. First, though, she'd have a shower. She kicked off her shoes and made for the bathroom, removing her hijab as she did so.

After her shower she dressed, and taking a key from a kitchen drawer, went down the stairs and opened the door of the flat below. Wrinkling her nose in disgust at the smell, she turned on the light and saw a scene like the ones that kept her awake at night, and troubled her dreams when she slept. As if in a trance she moved over to the drinks cupboard and opening it, felt inside. The message wasn't there. When she turned around she was facing what she knew would come one day – someone pointing a gun at her they meant to use. She was grateful that she'd replaced her hijab after her shower, for a headscarf was a fitting thing for a woman to wear where she hoped she was going.

The quiet of the morning was shattered for an instant by the shot, but the echoes faded, and the silence soon returned, descending like fine dust to settle everywhere in the flat. Hanson looked down at the body without emotion, and felt in his pocket for the message she'd come to retrieve, from the drinks cupboard. He looked at the Arabic script for a moment detailing the final plans for the bombings, and ordering his execution. He smiled. He was to be killed to prevent him giving away information to the Brits, but he'd never have shared anything with them, anyway, surely they knew that? He'd trusted them, but they'd betrayed him. They'd know how much he resented that when they found their dead girl. He wondered who they were going to use to kill him, and found that he didn't really care.

Hanson limped over to the window and gazed out for a while. Then he crossed to the drinks cabinet and poured himself a whisky. He downed it in one, and held up the glass to the light, as if toasting something. He moved to the window again and looked out. He saw the slender branches of the trees stirring uneasily in the bitter east wind, the damp mist from the river pouring pale white across the park and noticed that a thin rain was beginning to fall. *One more drink*, he thought, and then he'd really have to go.

BEYOND THE GRAVE

Captain Simon Seymour was driving the Humvee when it ran over the landmine and the last thing he remembered seeing was the British cemetery bordering the road. It was also the last thing he saw with both eyes, for he lost one of these and a foot, before hitting the ground. The vehicle had veered off the road, crashed through some railings, bounced twice and smashed into a row of gravestones. When the medics reached the wreckage they found Simon, the only survivor, more dead than alive, sprawled across three gaping graves whose stones had been shattered by the impact.

No longer fit for active combat duties he left the army and returned to his old university to carry out research into English Civil War skirmishes in the South Midlands. The aftermath of conflict had always intrigued him, and now, he reflected ruefully, he had personal experience of war's cost to human life. After his doctorate he worked for an association responsible for British military cemeteries, both in the UK and abroad. About the time he started the job he began dreaming of graves.

That didn't affect his work, which was varied and interesting. One day he could be in the field authenticating a soldier's grave in France, the next writing an article on mediaeval sites and a few days later surveying damaged obelisks to the fallen in Aden. The 'fallen' is what he always called the dead, for it gave dignity to a soldier's death and much-needed succour to the relatives, when the reality, in the First World War at least, was a bewildered child dying in a filthy foxhole, screaming for his mum.

To his surprise, Simon found aspects of the job moved him deeply – like finding a tiny cemetery with a wall and archway designed by Lutyens in a peaceful meadow in France commemorating Chinese workers who fell in the Great War. But the desecration of cemeteries, especially abroad, and the insensitive behaviour of tourists in the presence of grieving relatives, disturbed him greatly.

Since his accident, Simon discovered more and more of this side of himself that he hadn't suspected existed. Now he felt privileged in being able to assist grief-stricken people reach closure after loss, and guide others in drawing a line under long-standing issues. It also helped him come to terms with his own injuries, and learn how to live with the loneliness of being a deserted, divorced husband.

His condition had also kindled in him a love of the English countryside, and he enjoyed visiting local churches on field trips. He sensed the deep 'rightness' of an 800-year-old building built close to the people of its village, or alone in a meadow, early victim but now survivor of long-gone enclosures.

He warmed to churchyards even more than churches with their ancient yews framing the path from the lynch gate to the church. Although he'd made a study of the different designs on the headstones, it was the intimate little inscriptions and the faded plastic flowers spilled from their cheap glass vases that moved him to sadness and sympathy. Local craftsmen and their work intrigued him greatly, the carvings and lettering on rural gravestones as telling to him as any signature, that here was the work of a person skilled beyond the ordinary. *How much unrecognised talent resided in these places*, he thought, but how valued was the effect of its skill and care on those suffering loss and the pain of separation.

All through his early years working with war cemeteries, his dream never varied much. He was in a churchyard, listening to a voice coming from the ground which told him at first to accept and listen, and later told him to prepare. For what he had no idea. But a recurring dream over several years loses its power to shock, and he never felt the need to look for help, even if he'd known where to seek it.

One day Simon heard that local archaeologists, excavating Roman remains beside a church in South Oxfordshire, had come across a burial site from the Civil War, and knowing of his interest in the period invited him to come and inspect the dig. He arranged to meet the archaeologist in charge, and found nobody was working on the excavations when he arrived. But it was hard to feel aggrieved on a fine summer's day, especially when he'd taken a few days off to explore a lovely part of Oxfordshire.

The Thames ran past the church and upstream was the site of a medieval abbey, whose later chapel and buildings were still intact. Simon, unfamiliar with the church, saw at a glance that it was authentic and rare, having been spared the heavy hand of Victorian 'improvement'. And for some reason he felt drawn to it and the adjoining graveyard.

He took a room in the village pub, half a mile away, and searched for details of the church on his computer. Pevsner had a brief, bloodless entry, the county history a paragraph or two, and the local historical society had produced a printed booklet in the 1950s. The paucity of information was no surprise, and he'd often found it was better to get in touch with the local vicar. Or had been. Now team vicars often lived miles away from their churches, and when you wanted to see her, she was on maternity leave or taking a sabbatical in Walsingham. No longer would some scholarly, ancient incumbent take your arm and lead you round his church, pointing out the features he'd spent a lifetime and gallons of ink writing about in long-defunct publications. Where were they now? Somewhere in the sacristy, on a dusty shelf among water-stained vases full of dead flies, mildewed hassocks and old copies of *Hymns Ancient and Modern* with sun-curled covers? So much devotion, skill and love, forgotten and wasted.

Simon ran a busy, brisk young curate to ground in the nearest town, and asked if he might view the locked church and examine the stones in the churchyard more closely. The young man suggested that he should speak to the retired vicar, the Reverend Abne, who held a key, and as the church was unused, he could see no objection to the request.

Simon found the vicar in his garden, and after introducing himself, said, "I'd very much like to visit the church and read the citations of the gravestones in the churchyard. Some are very overgrown, would you mind if I cleaned them up?"

The vicar looked uncomfortable. "Dear me, hasn't Mr Purgess just done that?" he said.

"I hardly think so," said Simon, recalling the inscription on a grave by the lynch-gate.

"But the graves, the graves, they mustn't be damaged or the..."

"Contents disturbed in any way?"

"Quite so."

"If I removed the ivy from one or two, you could see how careful I am," said Simon, gently.

"That won't be necessary... Dr Seymour," said the vicar, glancing at his business card. "I'll give you the key to the church, but do take care not to *disturb* anything in the graveyard. And be sure to make yourself known to the canon in the abbey, you'll find he has certain responsibilities..."

Later in the day Simon drove to the church, got out and looked around. A copper beech beyond the churchyard was sharply outlined against the darkening blue of the sky, the trees overlooking the river were becoming hazy in the gentle evening light, and a light breeze from the water carried the sharp scent of mown grass, softened by the warmer scents of blossom. Water fowl were flying low over the river as swarms of gnats rose from the water's edge, bats fluttered through the fading light and rooks settled down noisily for the night in the trees. Apart from that nothing disturbed the deep silence of the place.

Simon pushed open the door of the church and walked inside. It was gloomy inside but reluctant to turn on the lights, he left, closing the door behind him, and stood in the porch looking at the graveyard. In front of him was a gravel path leading from the church to a gate in a low wall parallel to the river, and six gravestones set out in two rows to the left of the gate, with a single gravestone closer to the church. Many of the other graves were covered with bright green ivy, but on some stones an ochre-coloured lichen, dry and scaly, had taken over.

He was anxious to begin work, and seeing that it was still light enough to start, went to the car and collected some tools. He carried them back, set them out on the ground and started working on the lone sarcophagus near the six graves close to the wall. Only the gentle scraping of his trowel broke the silence.

"Bit late for you, Edwin," said a voice with a hollow tone. Startled, Simon looked up, and glanced around, but saw nothing.

"Actually it's Simon Seymour," he said, lamely.

"Ah, *actually* arrived, at last," said the voice.

Simon put his ear to the gravestone. "Are you in there?" he whispered. "Who are you, and how do you know me?"

"Yes," came the reply, "and word gets about. What does it say on the gravestone, son?"

"C.V. Hale, 1817–1882."

"Now you know who you're talking to. Go over to Mr Hardy, there's a good lad, and tell him what you're doing."

"Mr Hardy?"

"Marble gravestone, big angel on top, one wing chipped. Tell him I didn't ask you to start with me."

Simon surprised himself by taking all this quite calmly. When he found the grave Mr Hale had described, he put his lips close to the stone, and spoke softly. "Mr Hardy, are you there?"

"Where else would I be, *when* I'm here?" said a deep voice.

"I'm cleaning Mr Hale's sarcophagus. I'm to tell you he didn't ask to be done first."

"Half finished already, though, I'll be bound. That's a Black Death Club member for you."

"I don't know anything about that, and I don't want to upset… anyone," said Simon, "but I've never had any dealings with—"

"The 'dead'. That's what you were going to say, wasn't it, *Doctor* Seymour. The 'late lamented', 'extinct' more like, the way we're treated."

"How do you know my name?"

"Had our eye on you for a while now, Simon. It is Simon, isn't it? Especially now there's a vacancy."

"A vacancy? What vacancy?"

"Have a word with old Hale about that, seeing as he's a member of the Black Death Club. That's all for now, *Simon*."

Simon returned to the grave he'd started cleaning, knelt down and addressed the cold stone.

"Speak up!" said Mr Hale.

"Mr Hardy said I should ask you about the vacancy," Simon said. "And something about you being a member of the Black Death Club."

"Eaten up with envy, that being."

"How is it you both seem to know me?" asked Simon.

There was a pause. "Because you've got the talent, that's why. Not many like you – one less now."

"What talent?"

"The ability to *commune,* what else?"

"Is the vacancy to replace someone else who 'communed'?"

"Derek. Had the gift, but got too clever, wanted the three of us to 'integrate'."

"What did he mean by that?"

"Simon, listen carefully and don't forget I'm only telling you this because you've been *chosen*."

"By whom and for what?"

"Who knows, no one tells us anything down here. The forgotten ones, that's us."

"What 'three'?"

"The types down here. First there are the 'lifers' – the newly departed, not yet ready to move on. Then one day they feel the urge and pouf, gone! Then there's us 'lingerers'. Not many of us, and we could move on, but stay around. Don't ask me why."

"And the third?" asked Simon, "you said there were three."

"The 'malingerers'. Steer well clear of those boys and girls, Simon, or you'll end up…" His voice faltered and weakened, and then there was silence.

Simon returned to Mr Hardy's grave and, in reply to his enquiry heard a faint voice say, "You'll be contacted… tonight and…" and more silence.

He packed up and drove back to the pub. That evening when he came down from his room, the landlord gave him an envelope inside which was a note from a Canon Knollys of the nearby abbey, asking Simon to meet him at his residence at nine o'clock the following morning.

The next day he knocked on the door of the pretty Dower House, Jacobean, with later additions, and surrounded by well-kept gardens. Canon Knollys, late sixties, lined and freckled, with scanty sandy hair, light blue eyes and an anxious, darting manner, met him at the door and ushered him through a cool, dark passage, smelling of old wood, beeswax and metal polish. Simon followed him into a book-lined room with mullioned windows overlooking the abbey gardens. The canon motioned for him to take an armchair by the side of the fireplace, and sat down facing him.

"Dr Seymour," he began, "I'm obliged to you for our meeting at such short notice."

"Not at all, there's no problem about my work in the graveyard, I hope?"

"Your efforts do have a bearing on the reason for our meeting, for they led to some unexpected conversations, I believe."

"You mean my contact with the dead?"

Canon Knollys, began cleaning his spectacles vigorously, for his was a gentle world of innuendo and inference, and he found such direct speech uncomfortable. Having regained his composure, he said, "The site of the repositories to which you have alluded, to wit, the churchyard, is under my... jurisdiction. And, in your case, for some reason a portion of the veil has indeed been lifted, and you have been permitted a *glimpse* of the 'other side'. Oh dear, I hope that doesn't sound *too* severe."

Simon hated to see anyone distressed. "Have you considered what a compliment it is to your ministry here, Canon Knollys, that those interned here, have been granted the gift of tongues to speak to one of the living?"

The cleric brightened up. "One has always done one's *best*, not, of course, in the hope of... reward," he said, rubbing the inside of his clerical collar vigorously, his cheeks reddening with pleasure. "And please address me as Edwin, we must strive to be *modern* about such things."

"How is it that I can communicate with these... people?" asked Simon.

"Any dreams, after a traumatic experience, near a cemetery?"

"Yes," said Simon, inclined to add, "as well you know."

"That is one sensitising route, as we say."

"I haven't upset anything concerning your... parishioners, have I?" said Simon.

"There's no problem with your involvement, at all," said Edwin, "quite the contrary. Indeed, it is we who must confess to causing you embarrassment."

"I'll help if I can," said Simon, "but please don't get me into something I can't handle. I've a feeling I could be taking some flak from these... people."

Edwin, too young to have been a chaplain in Bomber Command during the war, which he bitterly regretted, knew all about flak. "Don't alarm yourself on that score," he said, cheerily, "help will always be at hand."

"So what's the problem?"

"Disruption and dispossession."

"Meaning?"

"The churchyard," said Edwin, "*your* churchyard, Simon. So close to the river... so very beautiful, but now subject to a land drainage project. A large pipeline has to go through a part of the graveyard."

"I see," said Simon.

"Only a section of the graveyard would be affected, and the bishop agrees that we must go along with the proposal. It's a long-*established* parcel of ground, and there are no known relatives to contact or endowments to maintain the graves."

"Where will the pipeline run?"

Edwin beckoned him over to his desk, took a sheet of squared paper from a drawer and spread it out. It was a map of the churchyard with the graves neatly numbered, and across the lower quarter of the plan a diagonal line had been drawn.

"You see the ones involved," Edwin said, pointing at the seven graves set apart from the rest. "Of course, the sarcophagus on its own is Hale's. That's number one, and Hardy's grave is number four."

"And the others involved?"

"We know who *should* be there," Edwin said, "but frankly we don't know who's there now. You've established a 'rapport' with two of our... ex-parishioners, and we were wondering if you might introduce the topic we've been discussing to them? And a list of current... residents would be invaluable."

"I could try," Simon replied, wondering to whom the 'we' referred. "Who should I contact first?"

"With whomsoever you feel most comfortable," said the canon, "but *please,* proceed with a degree of caution."

"Edwin, you and your colleagues are more experienced at this sort of thing than me," Simon persisted, "and you're professionals. Why use me for the job?"

"You're youngish, fresh and have the gift," he said. "Older

people lose that edge – like sniffer dogs, so they tell me. And you've got the 'wavelength', as the boys in the Diocesan Graveyard Squad call it. To be frank, those below ground don't listen much to me. I've lost what is rather vulgarly called 'coffin cred', and it's time for new blood. Speaking wholly metaphorically, of course," he added hurriedly.

"When should I start?" Simon asked. "Is there a good time to make contact?"

"Evening," Edwin said, firmly, "always the best time. We'll close the churchyard whilst you're 'working it', as we say. Perhaps you might start at eight o'clock tonight, reception's usually good then. And may we convene here tomorrow morning, at 9.30? Then you'll meet a colleague of mine, but we needn't go into that at the moment."

He saw Simon to the door, and as he left, gripped his arm. "It's just like being in the war, seeing the chaps off on another mission," he said wistfully, reviving his dream of sending pilots to their likely deaths with a spirited homily ringing in their ears. "Good luck m'boy!" Simon walked thoughtfully away.

★ ★ ★

When he reached the churchyard, shadows were lengthening over the grass and the light was fading. Now there was no breeze to freshen the air, clouds of gnats drifted listlessly beside the river's margin, and even the leaves of the horse chestnuts seemed to droop with fatigue. The gates to the churchyard had been padlocked, and Simon was quite alone.

He'd decided to speak to Mr Hardy and sat down facing his grave, carefully placing a voice recorder on the stone. "Are you there?" he called softly. There was no reply, and around him the little world of the churchyard continued preparing for the night. Then he heard a faint noise, tensed and leaned forwards.

"Simon." It was the same voice but much fainter.

"Mr Hardy?"

"What news?"

Simon felt uneasy. "How are you?" he asked, lamely.

"What's going on up there?" said the voice. "Get on with it."

"I hope Mr Hale won't mind me speaking to you, first."

"He's away. On a grave-swap. Last minute offer. He'll be in Australia, by now."

"A grave-swap?"

"You swap houses, we swap graves. That all right with you?"

"Yes, yes, but if I need to reach him what should I do?"

"Tell Edwin Knollys and he'll send him an email. That's 'ethereal mail', not some primitive electronic system."

"Are you serious?" said Simon.

"My boy, you're new to all this," Hardy said, kindly. "Things are very different down here from your world. For example I'm not 'here' as much as 'many-where', which, of course, isn't the same as 'anywhere'. Incidentally that device of yours won't record anything, because it won't pick up my vibrations. Now, what have you to tell me?"

Simon cleared his mind, said he'd spoken to Canon Knollys, outlined the proposed pipeline plan and Hardy listened in silence.

"They don't know up there who's in those gravesites," continued Simon, "can you help, please? And do your... neighbours really mind where they 'live'?"

"Of course they do. When others move on, lingerers may be offered a different gravesite, and the most sought after are the seven where this new pipeline will run. Now I'll go through the occupants' names, and make sure you get them right."

When he'd finished, Hardy laughed, "That should please Edwin. I expect he told you they'll be someone else there when you reported back?"

Simon nodded. "Yes, but he didn't say who."

"It'll be William Sneath, the 'witch-finder general'."

"It's so confusing," said Simon, miserably.

"Don't lose heart, and don't forget you're special. Few of

the living can do what you're doing, and there's usually a good reason for it. But watch your step, and don't trust anyone, not Sneath or Knollys, or even me! We're all pulled in a number of ways that even we don't always understand."

"Thanks for being honest! " said Simon.

"Not at all. Let me know what they say tomorrow evening."

★ ★ ★

At 9.30 the next morning Simon knocked on the door of the Dower House. Edwin opened the door and led him along to the study where a tall, gaunt man in a dark suit was standing, gazing out of the window. Deep in thought, he started slightly when they entered the room and turned to face them.

"Dr Seymour," said Edwin, "may I introduce you to the archbishop's spiritual advisor, William Sneath?"

The man surveyed Simon from his great height and extended a pale, bony hand, his sallow features creasing into a mirthless smile, quickly replaced by a scrutiny of profound penetration. His eyes were remarkable, black and glittering as if lit by some intense inner fire.

"Ah, Dr Seymour," he said, in a deep voice to which clung vestiges of his native Northern Ireland, "we meet at last. Your gifts will be of great benefit to us, I am sure. Now, let us to business, without delay."

"Before we do, I must tell you that I haven't the faintest idea of what's going on, or what's expected of me," said Simon.

Sneath fixed him with his burning gaze. "My dear Doctor, do not be alarmed. If I might permit myself the indulgence of offering you advice, it is essential that you garner a little more experience before receiving further explanations. And so now, with your forbearance, may we now turn to the substance of your discussion with Mr Hardy?"

"There's another thing."

"Well?"

"My dream."

"What about it?"

"Last night I saw the voice."

"What exactly did you see, Simon?" asked Edwin, quietly.

"I was in a dark place, like a narrow passageway, the walls were glistening, as if running with damp. There was an earthy smell, and I felt trapped and panicky. This figure came towards me, in a kind of mist, wavering and grainy like the image on an old film. And when it spoke it was the voice in my dream. It was so odd to *see* someone speaking to me, using such familiar tones."

"Can you describe the figure?" asked Edwin.

"A man, middle aged, short, fattish, shiny bald head."

"Full white beard?"

"Yes."

"This him?" said Edwin pulling out an ancient photo album from a drawer, holding it open, and pointing at a faded, brown photograph.

"Yes."

"Did he say anything?" said Sneath.

"We need you here. You must come here, now."

"Is that all?"

"Yes, over and over again, and then it faded away. Who was it?"

"C.V. Hale. No living layman has ever seen what you have. I suppose you know that he's in Australia now on some wretched sabbatical."

"Grave-swap, " Simon said. "It was a grave-swap."

"*Grave-swap*? That's a new one on me," said Edwin. "Have you heard of anything like that, William?"

"No, I have not," Sneath replied. "What on earth is Cyril Hale up to?"

"He went because something terrified him," said Simon. "I know the feeling! And what's this about wanting me there? I don't want to go anywhere. Certainly not where Hale was speaking from! It was horrible!"

"It was only because he projected the image of his anxiety on to you. You'd find it quite pleasant elsewhere," said Sneath. "But let's leave that aside for a moment and turn to Hardy. Tell us what he said."

Simon took a deep breath. "He gave me a list of the names of those affected by the proposed pipeline, and said that I was to trust nobody."

Sneath, ignoring the remark, suggested that they first re-examine the layout of the churchyard, and they bent forward to check out the detail.

"The occupants need careful handling," said Edwin, " and we *must* persuade them to vacate the graves. Before the pipeline goes through we must deconsecrate the land, and if anyone's *in situ* then, that gives others... opportunities. Dear God," he said, with a shudder, "if some things down there get wind of what we're trying to do..."

"Oh, you mean the malingerers," said Simon, "what could they do?"

Edwin had gone white as a sheet, and Sneath came to the rescue.

"They are unpleasant rather than evil entities, and their influence is relatively limited," he said, "and we're not entirely powerless in such matters, but it would be better if we could effect a smooth transition. Once the residents have left their current dwellings, I will perform a ritual to prevent any unwanted intrusion."

"It's not all sweetness and light down there, is it?" said Simon, who had a nasty feeling what was coming next.

"It's true that each occupant *flavours* their environment with their own feelings and personality," said Edwin, "and just like us their moods vary depending on their circumstances."

"Simon, remember Hale," said Sneath. "He's basically a jolly enough irritant, but something frightened him so much that he decanted to Australia. And, as I said you were affected by his last fearful feelings and the residues of his anxiety."

"You're going to ask me to go down there, aren't you?" said Simon, "To help sort out this lot, with their flavours and residues. With malingerers at every turn."

"Scarcely *every* turn, my dear Simon," murmured Edwin, "*occasional* sightings perhaps, and even those at a safe distance."

Sneath, growing impatient, then asked Simon to identify the occupants of each of the seven graves and, when he'd finished, suggested they tackled the problem of each in order. They started with Hale.

"He may be in Australia *spiritually* but formally he's still in number one," said Edwin. "And it's empty at present, so I suspect this 'grave-swap' nonsense was a smokescreen."

"And let's not forget he has occupational rights to a Black Death Grave, as well," said Sneath. "Simon, you've seen him with fresher eyes than ours, what do you make of him?"

"He's self-important, and obsessed with getting his own way."

"I agree," said Sneath, "so how do we deal with him?"

"Give him what he thinks is power and influence. Anything with an impressive title – spiritual envoy to an African archbishop would be good, or how about roving advisor to the General Synod? Or a sinecure with a fancy title in a cathedral? I imagine there are lots of those."

"True enough," said Sneath, with a smile. "I don't think we need to bother you with that one, Simon. And we'll make the offer of a post conditional on him giving up his Black Death Grave rights. Now for graves two and three."

"Joshua and his wife Emily Tooker are in number two, and Charlotte Nesbitt's in number three," said Edwin. "Victorian neighbours in earthly life, devout churchgoers, and long overdue to move on."

"Perhaps they just like being lingerers," said Simon.

"Joshua's not happy down there at all," said Sneath. "Some disharmony, I understand."

"Anyway, Charlotte Nesbitt will do whatever Emily Tooker

does," said Edwin, "and they'll all do what the bishop tells them to do. William, can you get on to him to drum up some episcopal rubbish on a parchment to help them on their heavenly pilgrimage? Simon, can give it to them when I've briefed him? When he's back, in a few minutes, we can get on with the others."

"How can I be back so soon," stammered Simon, "when you've got to get a document from the bishop and instruct me? And you haven't even asked me if I'll go… down there, yet!"

"Come with me," said Edwin, and led the way into the sunlit abbey gardens where they sat together on a bench. "To answer your last question first," he said, "you know you will help. Do you think your dream was nothing but idle fantasy? And the voice nothing more than empty speech? And are you not already familiar with something of the world you are about to enter?"

"I am afraid," said Simon.

"My dear boy, that's why we want you to have your first experience with these simple Victorians," said Edwin, "with you armed with the means to propel them to a higher level of existence."

"Is the process… painful at all?" asked Simon.

"Not at all," said Edwin, and lightly touched his forehead.

"I see he's gone," said Sneath, who'd walked over to join Edwin.

"An easy transition, thank God," said Edwin. "You never know…"

★ ★ ★

Simon was no longer in the garden, but where was he? He didn't know, for he was surrounded by a dark mist. And what a smell! It was like nothing he'd experienced before, but what was it? He identified soot, sweat and sewage, horse manure, grease and glue.

The mist dissipated and he looked about him. He was in a street, covered in horse dung, with a row of neat, newish terraced houses facing him, and holding a roll of parchment sealed with wax. Somehow he knew he must go to the house directly in front of him, and he limped up the steps, and knocked on the black-painted door. The door was unlocked and, getting no reply, he pushed it open and looked inside.

It was gloomy but he could make out highly patterned tiles on the floor, dark skirting boards, flock wallpaper to the dado rail and large floral paper on the upper walls. There was a hall table with a mirror, an aspidistra in a jardinière and framed needlework invocations to God hanging from the picture rail. A dark red runner covered the centre of the flight of stairs to his left, and in front of him was a brown door, slightly ajar.

Beyond the doorway he found a parlour with a cast-iron fireplace, in which a coal fire was burning with a smoky, sullen glow. The mantelshelf above was festooned with ornaments, and on either side of the fire were two over-stuffed armchairs with buttoned backs. The atmosphere in the room was stuffy and stale, and fine black coal dust lay like powder on every surface. The smell from the street was now replaced by a sharper scent of carbolic soap, starch and sweat.

On either side of the fire sat a couple whilst, in a corner, sat a woman on a balloon backed chair before a small table. The man, in his sixties, had a mane of white hair, large mutton-chop whiskers, and was dressed in a frock coat and waistcoat with a large watch chain. Both of the women had straight hair, parted in the centre, wore voluminous dowdy dresses with high necklines and looked severe.

They all regarded him calmly, and apart from the context and their dress, appeared quite normal to Simon, who'd expected wavering, grainy images. But everything became horribly strange when the man opened his mouth and spoke, for his voice sounded like an old recording, the words booming and distorting, out of synch with his lip movements. Simon craned forwards to catch the words.

"Sir, you have come, as we knew you would," said the man.

"The injured, kind one, the messenger carrying news from above."

"Mr Tooker?" said Simon. The man stiffened and the women shrank back holding their hands to their ears. Simon lowered his voice to a whisper, and the others relaxed. "Sir, I bring good tidings, for you and for Mrs Tooker, too."

The man pointed to the woman sitting alone at the table, who nodded primly. There was an awkward pause, and Simon, thrown off balance stammered, "And Miss Nesbitt, of course." The woman beside the man gave a brief smile.

"And here, from the hand of your bishop, is a passport to higher things, a happy release," said Simon, giving the parchment to the man with a flourish.

"Good news indeed, and the time is ripe. We are happy that it is you who has come to guide us on our way, God bless you," said the man. "Ladies, let us take our leave, and start our joyous journey."

He stood up and shook Simon's hand and the women curtsied before him. Then they all withdrew, linked hands and were gone. And Simon was back in the abbey garden, with Edwin sitting beside him on the bench.

"How did you find your first descent?" Edwin asked.

"Everything happens so quickly," gasped Simon.

"Time is relative, is it not? The Tookers have gone, I take it?"

"Mr Tooker and Charlotte Nesbitt, accompanied by Emily Tooker, have indeed, been despatched," said Simon, with a grin.

"Really," said Edwin, mildly. "Well done, that's three graves accounted for, leaving four to go. Let us go now and see William Sneath who, I believe, we'll find in the study."

★ ★ ★

Sneath greeted them and offered Simon his congratulations. "Whilst you were away we selected a suitable position for Mr Hale, which I'm pleased to say he accepted," he said, "and he surrendered his rights to a Black Death grave site, and now he's on his way back to England."

"Now for number four," said Edwin briskly, "that's Ron Hardy, of course."

"Any thoughts, Simon?" said Sneath.

"He was envious of Hale's membership of the Black Death Club," said Simon, "and you keep referring to it, but you've never told me what it is."

"A lot of nonsense, no provenance for it, whatsoever," said Edwin. "Graves get disturbed over time and a rumour started down there that some graves near the porch had got bones in them dating back to the Black Death in the fourteenth century. Someone then started a club whose members had rights over these graves."

"As well as the ones they were occupying?" Simon asked. "That doesn't sound fair."

"That cuts no ice with lingerers," said Sneath, "it's the status of 'old bones', you see, rather like 'old money' up here."

"What do they do in this club of theirs?" asked Simon.

"They 'network', isn't that what they call it nowadays? Play bridge, have dinner parties and sex orgies, for all I know or care. It's all in their minds, of course. But membership's limited, because the number of graves is fixed, so it's *exclusive*."

"Dead men's shoes, then," said Simon, laughing.

"Please be serious," said Edwin, wearily. "Anyway, we can offer Hardy the Black Death site that Hale has given up, and he can vacate number four."

"I'll do that, leave it to me," said Sneath who left the room. When he returned he said, "That's all settled. In fact he's already moved in and is as happy as—"

"An angel with four wings!" said Edwin.

"Do let's get on," said Sneath, "it's nearly lunch time, and I'm famished!"

"Number five. That's Mr Pryke," said Simon, looking at his notes, and wondering about the world he'd entered.

"Pryke the hypochondriac!" Edwin exclaimed. "He was one of mine, when I was a novice psychic case cleric. A master of deception, and with me it was hypochondria. If he had the driest grave he'd say it was running with damp, if there was night duty on All Souls' Night he'd be running a temperature. Never showed up at Halloween, and as for malinger watch patrol, forget it!"

"So how do we get him to move?" Sneath frowned.

"William, you're not going to like what I'm going to suggest," said Edwin. "I want to put him in the abbey vault – there's space under the nave since the abbot moved on."

"Are you serious, man? The Tudors will go mad."

"Let them, the abbey's in my care, and I'm fed up with that damned upstart, Sir Periam Costym, and his fishwife of a lady. Not to mention their thirteen brats – at least they've left the home tomb. The pair are just empty vaulters and they've lived like that for nigh on 400 years. It's high time they had company, and they can just put up with Pryke's sniffles, or whatever part he's currently playing. And Simon can tell him that from me!"

Sneath looked doubtful. "Do you think he's ready?"

"Yes," said Edwin.

"Well, if you're really sure, brief him."

"Excuse me but I am here, you know," said Simon.

"Of course you are, and ready to help, God bless you," said Edwin.

"I'll do it, of course," said Simon, "but I'd like to be back for lunch!"

"Rome wasn't built in a day, you know," said Edwin, with a twinkle in his eye. "Tell Pryke about the new heating system in the abbey and the status of living there, emphasise the peace and quiet." He touched Simon on the forehead and said, "Off you go!"

Again the mist, but this time it was not a smell that assaulted his senses but a feeling of utter misery and hopelessness that rolled over him. It was like a clammy thick fog, sliding its way into a dank Scottish loch on a cold winter's evening. Why should he think of Scotland, he wondered, for he hardly knew the place. So why did he hate it so and see it as a dank breeding ground for horrid biting insects, populated by an ugly red-haired race of surly-spoken malcontents, bigots and sanctimonious self-seekers?

Wherever had these thoughts come from? he wondered, as the mist cleared. Then he gasped, for in the blink of an eyelid he'd come from the gentle warmth of a lovely southern garden to a dark, grimy street, covered in litter with a thin scattering of dirty snow, an icy wind chilling him to the bone and a mood of intense depression. He looked around and saw a rag and bone horse and cart in the road, a gang of scruffy boys vandalising an empty shop, a fifties car or two, and a grubby brownstone terraced house before him with a tarnished brass plate saying 'Doctor's Surgery'.

Using his stick to help him, he climbed up the cracked stone steps and pushed open the door. It was like a steam bath inside, and he felt stifled and sweaty. This was quickly overtaken by nausea as he was bathed in a sickly smell of surgical spirit, bay rum and oil of cloves, simmering together in an atmosphere as thick as rancid soup, rank with the smell of heated, steaming wet clothes and urine. He gasped again.

"Close that damned door," rasped a voice, muffled but penetrating. "A body could die from that draught!"

Simon looked across the room and saw the speaker was a cadaverous man, hunched up in front of a one-bar electric fire, wearing a filthy overcoat several sizes too big for him, with a grubby woollen scarf wound under his chin and over the top of his head. A white, blotchy, unshaven face, with watery, red-rimmed blue eyes peered at Simon, whilst the bloodless lips puckered in a snarl of complaint and irritation.

"Mr Pryke?" said Simon.

"Who wants to know?"

"My name is Simon Seymour, and I've come to—"

"Whatever you've come to do, forget it, one eye," Pryke butted in, with a laugh.

"This is not the place for someone in your condition," Simon said, trying not to mind the rudeness, "and that fire's not much help. You'll get chilblains, and judging from the sound of your voice, you need urgent medical treatment."

Pryke's eyes sparkled with malice, misery and self-pity. "I'm waiting for it," he cried, "I'm not in this stinking hole by choice, you know. But no one comes, no one ever comes."

"How long has it been?" Simon asked.

"Time! Time! What does that matter? Fifty human years maybe, maybe more. Feels like an eternity, waiting in this Scottish hell!"

"I know a place where you could be a lot happier," said Simon.

"Not a pokey bloody space in a new town up here, with 'mod cons' and bugger all culture. They've not even heard of Shakespeare up here, can you credit it?"

Was this a glimmer of hope there, thought Simon. He said, "What I can offer you, is a warm, sheltered, spacious, vaulted accommodation in an important medieval structure, private and secluded, but with the option of mixing, should you wish it, with a titled contemporary of William Shakespeare. He has resided there for several hundred years with his lady wife."

"Any kids?" asked Pryke. "Bloody Tudors bred like rabbits."

"A few, but all gone. Left the nest— vault, I mean."

"What's he like this Tudor?"

"Made his money through the meat trade after the army. Spent some time up here, I believe: 'Hammer of the Scots', that kind of thing."

"Oh, he was, was he? English bastard, trampling on the flowers of the forest. I'd like get my hands on him."

"I didn't realise you were so pro-Scottish. After all, it's your attitude that has created this world!"

"Scottish, born and bred, laddie. Tudor chap has a wife you say?"

"Before she was a lady she was a 'hostess' in a bear pit theme park."

"Interesting background for a lassie. Security of tenure if I move into this vault place?"

"Don't see why not. Could you leave at once?"

"Where is it?"

"Oxfordshire."

"Aye, laddie. Good riddance to this dump. Now back to the dreaming spires of me youth. Loud hurrahs."

Simon blinked and found himself in Edwin's dining room, where he was having lunch with William Sneath.

"Well?" said Sneath, looking up from his plate.

"Complicated man, this Pryke. Did you know he was Scottish?"

"Sometimes – when he's feeling ignored and hard done by. Did you find him in that awful doctor's waiting room in Glasgow?"

"Depressing."

"You should get him in Scott's tent in the Antarctic surrounded by dead bodies. Anyhow will he move?"

"I think so – if you confirm the security of his tenancy. Will you do that please?"

Edwin nodded. "I'll see to it. But I'll have to tell him there's only Lady Costym's there now. I lost my temper with her husband after umpteen years, and he took umbrage and went, leaving wife in the vault. On the cards for a few decades, apparently."

"I'm sure Mr Pryke will welcome her company, and he's ready to go when you give him the word."

Edwin looked vacant for a moment and then said, "It's done. Now come and have some lunch, and afterwards we'll sort out the remaining two graves."

★ ★ ★

"Now for the rest," said Sneath, when they were back in the study. "Old Erasmus is in number six."

"That's Heronimus St John Fitzwilliam, fellow and

201

sometime dean of All Saints, the Oxford College, 1723–42," Edwin explained.

"We did the college a favour in the Civil War in the seventeenth century by taking their silver into safekeeping, and housing some of their grave folk," said Sneath.

"For which they awarded us a 'Gravesite Emeritus' in their graveyard," said Edwin, "in perpetuity and in the gift of the incumbent of the abbey. That's me."

"I'm sure the old scholar would be delighted to return to his *alma mater*, to rest amongst former friends and colleagues," said Sneath.

"It shall be done," said Edwin.

Number seven was occupied by a Georgian sailor, Captain Gale, who died in a carriage accident on a turnpike whilst travelling to take up command of his ship in Portsmouth. A man, sad to be buried far inland, always longing for his last 'berth' within sight of the sea.

"Fancy a trip around the pier, Simon, a salty breeze in your nostrils?" said Edwin. "Captain Gale died in his prime, I doubt if he'll take much persuading to move if we get it right. But warning, malingerers have been sighted in the 'offing'. First William will find out what we can offer the old salt."

Sneath left the room and when he returned, reported that a vacancy for spirit commandant in residence had arisen at a gravesite near the Seaman's Mission in Portsmouth, and that the Lords spiritual at the Admiralty would accept his recommendation.

"Right, there you are, Simon, that should please him," said Edwin.

"How would I know someone was a malingerer if I met one?" Simon asked. "And how should I treat them?"

"If you do suspect someone, don't antagonise them," said Edwin. "And if it starts playing up, just *think* yourself here. If you get into real trouble, or need to do something important, just *will* it to be, and it will happen. Off you go now."

It was the usual mist, with a sharp breeze to blow it away, a smell of the sea and the sound of gulls wheeling above. Simon was alone on a darkening headland, far above a desolate coastline whose rocks were being pounded by heavy white waves. Below was the wreck of a three-master, rammed onto the rocks, battered by weather and waves, but still in one piece. Far out to sea he saw white sails, making towards a setting sun.

"Are you looking for the captain?" said a soft voice, behind him. He turned to face the most beautiful person he'd ever seen. It was as if all the features of all the women he'd met, liked or loved had been melded into one perfect face and figure. A great pang of hopeless longing, remorse and loneliness swept over him. He'd loved his wife with a tender passion from the moment they'd met and the love, for him at least, had deepened with time. And no woman had remotely attracted him since she'd left. But even the love for his wife would have paled beside what he was feeling for this woman.

"Yes, yes," he stammered, "do you know him? Is he near?"

"He can't get up here," she laughed. "I'm his eyes and his ears: I watch the ships sail by, I hear the wind in the grass on the cliff-top and the thunder of the waves on the rocks. I talk of such things and through me he never leaves the sea. And there's salt spray on my lips that he longs to taste. Would you? You can if you wish. Will you stay with me?"

"I must see him," said Simon. "You must tell me where he is."

"I'll take you to him, but then you and I will plan our life together, Simon. Come take my hand." They went down the cliff path, together, and he felt he was floating on air.

"Where is he?" he asked again.

"Near, near," she said, and the singing wind swirled in time with her words, and the world held its breath. When they reached the beach she pointed at the wrecked ship. "He is in there, and there he will stay. But we will not be mewed up like him, not us, Simon."

"I must see him," he said, "I must!"

"And I say no, you cannot," she shouted throwing down his hand.

"It is my *will* to see him," he said, fighting the emotions that wrapped his heart in loss and grief.

The girl's lovely face blackened with rage, and then became livid with anger. It changed again and again, and it was frightful to see. And then he was alone.

He reached the wreck and willed himself down into a dank, wooden prison. The oaken walls were running with slime, and the iron stanchions, loosened and hanging free, banged and echoed to the crash of waves smashing against them. Boom, crash, boom, crash. There was a stench of rotting seaweed and dead fish, rust and rotten wood, and in the corner, amidst the bedlam of noise, lay an enchained man, in ragged clothes on a bed of wet straw.

"Captain Gale," said Simon, "I've come to take you home."

★ ★ ★

"What did you make of your first malingerer?" said Sneath.

"I've never felt such longing for anyone," said Simon. "What would have happened if I'd gone with her?"

"You would have been chained to a rock of grief of your own making, full of pain and regret, like poor Gale. Until she moved on and then you'd be freed."

"Who was she?"

"Who knows? An unhappy soul. But your sailor's home and dry now, so to speak. And now, with the graves clear, we must decide on our next course of action. You must excuse us for a while, Simon, as we have many things to consider and plan."

★ ★ ★

A day later Simon was invited to a ceremony of 'protective deconsecration' and so, with the clerics in formal robes, he stood at midnight before Hale's former sarcophagus. Hale was in Wales conducting his duties as spirit plenipotentiary without portfolio in Llanduff Cathedral, the Tookers and Charlotte Nesbitt were singing in a heavenly choir, Hardy was organising a treasure hunt for the Black Death Club, Pryke was snug and warm in the nave of the abbey and the bosom of Lady Costym, Old Erasmus was at a Spiritual College dinner in his honour, and Captain Gale was gazing with rapture at the sea in Portsmouth.

William Sneath incanted, Edwin shook a shaky censer, everyone said "Amen", there was a brief flash, a slight shimmer of air over the graves and that was it. They all shook hands and Sneath said to Simon, "Many, many thanks. More harm than you can possibly know has been averted."

"Just like old times," said Edwin. "We won then, and we've won now." The two men turned and walked away, and Simon was left by the sarcophagus where it had all started. For a minute or two he stood in silence, and then he limped slowly away, through the churchyard.

"Oh, well *done,* Simon," said a thin, reedy voice, as he passed a large grave with the unpleasant lichen clinging to its sides. "Lucky this time, weren't we? Beginner's luck, do you think? *We* do. Not going to be so easy next time, *Simon.* We'll be waiting – you'll see."

Simon breathed heavily to steady himself, and feeling the need for a walk, began limping back through the dusk to the village where he was staying. He didn't hear the car coming up behind him, and it was early morning before a local found his body lying near the abbey. He ran to get Edwin Knollys, who called William Sneath.

Edwin was kneeling beside the body, tears streaming down his face when his friend arrived. He looked up, in distress. "First Derek, and now Simon. The car will never be traced, of course. Do we ask too much of them, William?"

"You know we are only sent those whose course is nearly run."

"Such sacrificial lambs, though, poor boys."

"Enough of that, Edwin. We'd better get Hale back from Wales, we're going to need him to help settle things with these damned malingerers. It's got to stop, it's bloody well got to stop! Before I'm finished with them, they'll wish they'd never died!"

"Well, at least we've got another ally on the other side to help," said Edwin mildly. "William, it's early days I know, but will you contact Simon tonight, or shall I?"